CHRISTMAS CHARITY

BEVERLEY OAKLEY

Copyright

Christmas Charity

First Large Print Edition

Copyright © 2020 by Beverley Oakley

CHAPTER 1

*C*harity shivered as she snuggled against Hugo's side, anticipation heightening as his gentle hands grazed her nipples.

Outside, the wind stirred the branches of the plane tree, its soft sighs competing with Charity's as tendrils of need speared her, even though it had been mere minutes since they'd collapsed, exhausted and satisfied, in each other's arms.

"Are you cold?"

The joyous strains of a group of Christmas carollers singing *Once in Royal David City* had made Charity shiver even more. This time with excitement for, with

Hugo by her side, she really could believe in "Peace on earth, and mercy mild, God and sinners reconciled."

"Here, my sweeting, I'll keep you warm."

Hugo always anticipated her needs, Charity thought dreamily as he drew her more tightly against him, her vision encompassing only his beloved, handsome face rather than the tawdry decorations of the room where she did her entertaining.

"I'm never cold when you're with me," she whispered, snuggling closer which blocked out the sight of the grimy curtains. Soon they would be a thing of the past. Like the shabby dresser, the faded blue satin counterpane, and the overdone gilt-edged paintings that decorated the place she'd called home for the past two years. Everything would be replaced by pieces exuding simple taste and elegance.

She'd have a bedchamber done up in blue and white like Lady Milton's, for whom her mother had worked as a governess when Charity had been a child. Charity had never seen such grandeur.

Charity's bedchamber, however, would

be equally hers and Hugo's; a place of happy trysting rather than formal and cold and barred to the master of the house which is how Charity's mother had explained the loveless marriage of her employers.

And Charity's little house would be as far away from Madame Chambon's House of Assignation as it was possible to be. Hugo had pointed it out to her during a carriage ride some weeks back, telling her it was as good as hers once the lease arrangements had been seen to. He'd given her carte blanche to decorate it as she chose, within certain limits, but he was as generous as any man alive. Dear lord but she was lucky. She shivered even more at the thought of their wonderful shared future and kissed Hugo's neck. "As long as you are with me, I can face any hardship."

His hand stilled and grew heavy on Charity's breast.

Charity glanced up at him.

"My darling, I have to tell you something."

The languorous contentment of just now was swept away by something difficult to read as his eyes clouded and his sweet gentle mouth formed a tight line. Raising her hand to his lips, he kissed her fingertips then sat up and swung his legs over the bed, hunched forwards and frowning as he clearly weighed up his next words.

The silence was heavy with portent. Charity braced herself as she watched him struggle. Her throat felt thick and it was suddenly difficult to breathe. Of course, it had been too good to be true. The man who'd taken her virginity; who'd kept coming back and whom she loved, now, with all her heart, was about to end the dream that she'd ever escape Madame Chambon's. His next words would destroy the illusion that love was possible for a girl who'd sunk as low as she had.

He twisted around, his expression torn, as if he didn't know whether to comfort her — for he extended his arm then dropped it — or keep the explanation short and brutal.

"Just tell me and don't spare my feelings," Charity muttered, balling her hands into fists as she lay rigidly on her back and stared between Hugo and the ceiling.

If she could only put up the casing to protect her heart that the other girls all described as their best defence in such moments, she might survive this but, truly, her heart had always been utterly unguarded with Hugo. He'd been such a loyal companion these past eighteen months. A true and loving companion who'd not stinted when it came to showing her in every way how much she meant to him.

Whereas she, Charity, had so little to offer in return.

Just her love, loyalty, and eternal gratitude.

And her body.

It was not a comforting reflection though, in truth, she couldn't see how else she'd have managed if she hadn't been taken in by Madame Chambon.

A girl had to make some hard decisions if she weren't to starve.

He swallowed, his face grey and drawn as he traced the outline of a flower on the counterpane. Or perhaps it was Charity's face, or her shoulder, or breast. Hugo had sketched just about every part of Charity with as much loving detail as he fashioned the words of the love poems which accompanied each drawing and poem he gave to her.

"Charity, I'm ruined." He closed his eyes briefly before fixing his gaze upon Charity. "There, I've been unable to put the truth so bluntly to anyone else, but that's the truth. Everyone has been in a state of quiet uproar because of my stupidity, and now I'm to be punished. I have to go away. My father has found me a position in the company in India." His mouth twisted.

"Ruined? You have to go to *India*?" Charity scrambled onto her knees and twined her arms around Hugo's neck. "How? Why?"

He stiffened. "Because I was a fool like I have never been before. I gambled away our future on the roll of the dice because I believed it would ensure we could be together forever. Always." He turned and cupped her face, his expression infinitely tender. "But I was burned. Just like my dreams of a future with you. Nothing but ashes."

"Oh, Hugo." Charity didn't know what

else to say. Hugo deplored gambling. What had induced him to do such a thing? And yet she didn't say it aloud. Hugo was suffering enough as it was.

He gripped her fingers. "I'd intended telling you this before I took you in my arms and we…went to bed." His tone was full of self-loathing. "But your greeting was so sweet, and just holding you seemed to give me the strength to face what I must — when I've wondered, these past days, how I'm going to manage to do that." His voice cracked. "Lord knows, it's hard enough to consider a position in India which would take me away from you for months. But to live there for up to two years?" He swallowed with difficulty. "My father's business interests in steel are prospering. His company is extending the railway line from Madras and he has decided that, as my punishment, I must oversee the project." A nerve twitched at the corner of his mouth. Otherwise, he was utterly composed. Only the tightness of his voice indicated his distress. "So, that is what I must do. I have no choice in the matter. The money my aunt left me, and which has enabled me to keep you while I enjoy a modicum of independence free of my father when he has such different plans for me — it's all gone. I am to accompany my Uncle Septimus." He closed his eyes, adding in a whisper, "Apparently, this will be my salvation."

"India?" Charity repeated. She could barely take it in. The future she'd dreamed of with the man she loved above all others had just been snatched away. But then, how could she ever have believed it was more than a dream? Girls like her had no right to believe in happiness.

Hugo stroked her face as he nodded. "God knows, I could face anything if I had you by my side. But it's impossible. I depart Southampton for Madras in less than a fortnight. My uncle, who was, I'm told, going to induct my cousin Cyril into the family firm, will instead be taking me under his wing."

Charity didn't miss the sarcasm. There was little love between Hugo and his forbidding uncle, or the cousin who was only a few months older than he.

"Couldn't I find a way to…to join you on the ship? To be wherever you are, Hugo?"

Hugo shook his head. "For the first few months, there'll be a great deal of travel around the country. It's no place for a woman, I'm told. Not that I could see you, anyway, as I'll be living with my uncle," he muttered.

The aching silence between them seemed to stretch forever; punctuated by the muted bumps and thumps from the other rooms.

"Oh Hugo, I…I don't know how I can part with you, my love." Charity hesitated. "Unless you wanted it."

"I will never be parted from you. Not forever. Not while I have free will!" With uncharacteristic fierceness, he gathered her in his arms. "I want you with me, always. I *need* you, Charity." He kissed her brow. "You make me whole, you make me feel alive. Only *you* do that." When he put her away from him, his sensitive face was taut with pain. "When you're with me, I can do anything; I'm the man I want to be. And I can paint. You're my magic."

"But your father has decreed that you go away. And...I can't go with you!" The shock was beginning to abate. Desolation was taking its place.

"You *know* my plan is to marry you as soon as I come into my inheritance."

"That's two years away, Hugo. Oh, my love, I don't know how I can bear it." The lump in Charity's throat was making it difficult for her to speak. Yes, Hugo had made it clear, right from the start of their relationship, that an honest, legal union between them was his goal the moment he was financially independent. His grandfather's fortune was to be split between him and Cyril upon their respective twenty-fifth birthdays. An aunt's modest bequest had enabled Hugo to keep Charity exclusively in the meantime.

But he'd lost that now. He was wholly dependent upon his father. And his father had no intention of his only son marrying a lowly, common creature like Charity. Even if it was he who had inadvertently been responsible for Charity and Hugo meeting after he'd forced his boy over the threshold of Madame Chambon's House of Assignation when he'd learned he was a virgin.

Like Charity had been.

Hugo gave a short laugh. "I never get tired of hearing you say that. Of calling me your love, your darling. My parents weren't exactly well-disposed to each other. No one calls anyone their love." His face clouded over again. "Except for grandmother, and that's because she was common. Besides, she's dead now. And Grandfather made all his money after he married her so she no longer has a place in the Adams' Family Lore."

Charity knew the story. Hugo's grandfather, a man of shrewdness and cunning, had made an unlikely fortune in the steel trade after starting life as a blacksmith. It was only natural each successive generation would marry up. Hugo's father had been courting a baronet's daughter when he'd been forced to marry the lowly solicitor's daughter he'd made pregnant. Hugo's mother.

A generation later and with even more coin in the family coffers, Hugo was to infiltrate the aristocracy. A penniless peer's daughter trading family lineage for Hugo's pocketbook was the plan.

Not an illegitimate governess's daughter living in a brothel.

Smiling, Hugo ran his fingers through her hair. "I didn't know what love was until I met you."

A wave of emotion threatened to engulf Charity. "Oh, Hugo, I wish I really *was* worthy of you!" she cried, hugging him tightly before drawing back.

"You mean, in my father's eyes." He traced her lips with his fingertips. "For I wouldn't change a thing about you, Charity, my love; only... my father holds the purse strings now." A muscle worked at the corner of his mouth. "And I sail in two weeks."

"Two weeks..." Charity felt the sting of tears, and the pain radiate throughout her body as if she'd been physically beaten by the news. "Two weeks and then I'll never see you again? Oh, Hugo, is there no other way?"

"I'd grasp it with both hands and the gratitude of a lifetime if only one could be found. But you *will* see me again." Getting to his feet, Hugo stood, naked and vulnerable by the bed where, once a week for the past eighteen months, Charity had experienced the only real love in her life. But there was no doubting his sincerity as he took her in his arms, kissed her gently on the lips and whispered, "I want you more than anything in the world, Charity."

And Charity believed he meant it when he vowed, "I swear that two years from now, on a wintry December morning, with the carollers warbling about peace on earth and mercy mild, I will marry you."

"And you will make me the happiest girl alive," Charity whispered.

Even though she knew such happily-ever-afters did not happen to girls like her.

CHAPTER 2

Feeling dull-eyed and hollow, Charity lowered herself onto the only remaining chair at Madame's crowded breakfast table and tried to eat.

She'd not been able to make the effort the previous day, but now her stomach felt hollow and she thought she would faint from lack of food.

Breakfast was habitually laid out at noon, and those girls too weary from the night before risked going hungry if they didn't present themselves. Madame wasn't inclined to indulge anyone. Except herself, of course. A pile of steaming, buttered crumpets piled onto a plate in front of her sent off an enticing aroma that would have made Charity's belly rumble with longing on any other day. Such treats were rarely for the girls, however. Plain bread and drippings were the mainstays of this first meal, but the fact that it was supplemented with porridge and eggs on an ad hoc basis was enough to draw most of the household's occupants downstairs.

"Hugo couldn't have been up to scratch with that long face, Charity," teased Emily. "Smile! You're the one who gives us hope in our own happily-ever-afters."

There were a few corroborating sighs at this. But Emily's remark was particularly painful this morning.

Unable to meet her eye, Charity slanted a glance at Madame. However, the steaming crumpets rather than Charity's response were occupying the complete attention of their benefactress.

Feeling sick with nerves, Charity decided this was as good an opportunity as any to speak the truth of her situation. If Madame was filling her belly with rich food, she might be more inclined towards leniency than otherwise.

"Hugo has to go away." She'd not meant to sound pathetic and lovelorn. Her voice was so soft, she wasn't even sure anyone heard her response, but suddenly all eyes were on her and a great many voices were asking, "What's happened, Charity? What do you mean, Hugo has to go away?"

Charity's throat felt swollen, like her eyes from the copious tears she'd shed the previous day and all night.

"But Hugo was never going to leave you. He's the one true faithful man who comes here. He can't do this to you! *Why* is he doing this to you?"

It was Rosetta, her voice growing shrill. Charity closed her eyes and wished the girl would calm down. It wasn't as if Hugo had left *her*.

"He lost heavily at the gaming table." There was no way to soften the truth. Charity sounded as bitter as she felt though she'd done her best to forgive Hugo.

"Oh, Charity, what will you do?"

Again, it was Rosetta, weeping, now, as if

her heart might break. Charity supposed she should feel more charitable towards her, knowing how badly treated she'd been by one of her clients in the past. She was damaged, her emotions always at the surface.

"Young Mr Adams has left you?" Only now did Madame raise her head and seem to take notice of the conversation.

In the light from the sun that slanted through the windows, Charity could see a droplet of honey clinging to an errant hair upon the woman's chin.

"He's said nothing to me, my girl."

"It was very sudden, Madame." Charity dropped her eyes as she waited for Madame to digest the implications. For her. For everyone. Charity no longer had a generous protector. Hugo was no longer able to pay for Charity's exclusive services as he had done for nearly two years.

Now, Madame would throw her to the wolves. She would make Charity available to all of her so-called discerning clients; and discerning depended on the fatness of their pocketbook.

She shuddered. Charity was about to become like Madame's other girls. She might be well fed and dressed but she'd have no choice as to whom she would sleep with any given night.

When she'd arrived, desperate and homeless, on Madame's doorstep, she'd had no idea such women even existed.

How much she'd learned since then.

And how miraculous to have escaped their fate.

Or, so she'd thought.

To her surprise, Madame spoke up, her voice thick with something that sounded more suspicious and thoughtful than the brusque dismissal that reminded Charity she could not expect to be treated with any special consideration.

"Perhaps that was the reason a certain Mr Cyril Adams darkened our doorstep with a request for your services last night, Charity." Madame dabbed delicately at her lips as she speared Charity with an incisive look. "I don't suppose you know him."

Charity drew in a quick breath but Patience, one of the older girls, let out a harsh laugh before saying with heavy irony, "What a charming piece that fellow is. Vain, selfish, and parsimonious, he is. Or, so I've heard."

"And also, Hugo's cousin," Charity said in a soft voice.

"I thought there was something havey-cavey going on," muttered Madame, tucking into another muffin before she'd finished her last mouthful of the first. "Though, of course, I had no idea your young Mr Adams had just given you up."

"He was going to marry me," Charity said softly. "Properly!" she added, before realising her error and casting an anguished look at her friend, Violet.

Violet, one of the most poised and beautiful young women at Madame Chambon's — in Charity's opinion — was about to embark on a sham marriage to a young lord. In fact, Charity herself would be present at the church as one of the witnesses.

Charity didn't miss the spasm of pain that crossed her friend's face. Quickly hidden, of course. Violet didn't reveal her feelings, though Charity knew Violet was deeply in love with young Lord Belvedere, an unlikely customer. A very dashing and charming one, too.

But a sham marriage was all it would be.

Violet patted Charity on the shoulder. "Please don't feel bad on my account. I never expected a proper marriage...but *you* were promised it and, knowing Mr Adams so well, as we all do, now, we had expected it."

"Indeed! It's not uncommon for true love to blossom under my roof — but for it to lead to *legal* marriage is a fine thing." Madame looked remarkably fiery as she pushed out her impressive bosom and stared down the table at the six girls gathered there. "I gave that cousin of Mr Hugo's short shrift, I can tell you." She shook her head, taking another mouthful as she added sorrowfully, "But now Mr Hugo has let you down, I don't know what will be done."

Charity didn't know either. Clearly, Madame would come up with something. She waited, holding her breath.

"You need not fear, Charity. I shall not sacrifice you to the first stranger who seeks your services. Not so soon after your terrible let-down. I have some compassion."

But you'd happily sacrifice me to the second within the week if his offer was good enough, Charity thought with more terror than bitterness.

The moment's silence suggested the other girls thought the same.

Until Rosetta said tentatively, "It would appear we are not the only ones who think poorly of Mr Adams."

As she was not one to voice opinions, the girls looked at her with surprise.

"Well, girl, you don't make remarks like that without backing them up," Madame barked.

Charity tried not to roll her eyes. This was not the approach to take with Rosetta if one wished for elaboration.

It was Violet who put her hand on Rosetta's arm and said gently, "What can you tell us about Mr Adams? Perhaps it's important in view of him poking his nose around here so soon after Charity's terrible disappointment." She sent Madame a significant look and Charity smiled gratefully. Violet was so calm and agreeable. She always knew what to say.

"The gentleman I entertained two nights ago said one of the few men in London he'd not game with was Mr Cyril Adams." She blushed and looked down. "But perhaps it's nothing. One can't believe everything a gentleman says."

"One certainly can't," Violet agreed. "But it is an interesting observation. Perhaps more than just a coincidence. What do you think, Charity?"

Charity nodded. Violet sounded so cultured yet she'd never divulged the real reasons she'd landed on Madame's doorstep several years before with nothing but a carpetbag of belongings yet looking and sounding every inch the well-heeled young lady. Violet had declared that she wanted to work as one of Madame's girls as if she'd really meant it and Charity, who'd been making her way along the passage, had been brought up short as she'd heard her declaration to Madame through Madame's half open study door.

"Hugo said his cousin had plied him

with drink then pressured him to play at dice." Charity could barely summon the energy to sit straight in her chair. "Hugo never plays. And he doesn't like his cousin. Oh lord, what would he do if he knew his cousin had come asking for me?" She managed to choke down the sob. "Is Mr Adams really that dreadful?" She shuddered at the thought of having to do with anyone what she'd done with Hugo. "I know they're competitive but — "

"Mr Adams is held in the highest *disregard*." It was Emily, now, adding her tuppence worth. "I heard from one of my fellers that Mr Adams palms cards and that's why *he'd* never play him."

"Mr Adams obviously cheated your Hugo!" Rosetta said but Charity shook her head. "Hugo rolled the dice with everyone watching him."

"The dice could have been loaded," Violet said.

"It is possible, Violet, to make dies that favours particular numbers." Rosetta glanced between Violet and Lizzie. "Perhaps you might make a few discreet inquiries amongst your gentlemen as to what else they know about Mr Adams and his enthusiasm for gaming." She looked over to Charity. "Perhaps we can uncover some misdeeds that will reverse Hugo's situation."

Charity's smile lacked conviction. With no independent funds, Hugo was in an impossible situation if his father was determined to send him out of the country.

Could she be the real reason? she wondered.

Could it be that she wasn't good enough for Mr Adams' son, and never would be?

As she tried to pay attention and be grateful for all the suggestions her friends were bandying around, the terrible thought kept running around her head: If Hugo hadn't lost his independence at the gaming table, would his father have found another means of separating them?

In which case, what hope was there for them to ever be together?

IT TOOK HUGO A FULL FIVE MINUTES TO PACE

the length of the long drawing room and back while he waited for his father to make an appearance.

How he hated this place and how glad he'd be to see the last of it. It was a house, not a home, with no evidence of a woman's touch since his mother had died so many years before.

No flowers in vases or paintings other than austere landscapes and portraits.

No feminine, decorative touches.

His father channelled his wealth into accoutrements that showcased his success, his power. Not his appreciation of culture for he had none. He'd been a lad when his father had amassed his fortune. Thomas Adams' own home had been modest for the first few years of his life, his schooling rudimentary. Success was based on grit and grind and, as far as he was concerned, anything soft or beautiful indicated weakness.

Of course, a potential wife from the upper classes might present herself as soft and beautiful but it would be her breeding papers that would concern Thomas Adams.

Having failed to fulfil his own marital

ambitions — Hugo knew this from the servants' whispers — Thomas Adams wanted just the right wife for his son. He'd go to his grave having overseen the Adams family's elevation from traders to aristocrats within his lifetime.

Hugo stopped by a wall of paintings. Landscapes and horses, mostly. Turners and Constables. It was Hugo's favourite room in the house but he doubted his father considered the artworks themselves. He'd bought them as investments.

Just as he'd seen it as an investment to nip Hugo's love of beauty in the bud by sending him off to boarding school.

However, a gruelling regime at Eton had only reinforced Hugo's hatred of vigorous pursuits rather than turning him into the man his father wanted him to be. Fencing lessons, pugilism bouts with the English heavyweight champion, and various other efforts to desensitise Hugo in the hope he'd develop manly interests and abandon his whimsies, had had the opposite effect.

Hugo moved to the end of the landscapes and stood facing a portrait of a pretty, finely dressed young woman standing by a horse. He supposed he shouldn't be surprised that his mother had been relegated to the shadows. His father never spoke of his late wife. She'd been a solicitor's daughter, too inferior to fulfil his marital ambitions, yet beguiling enough to entice Thomas Adams into a sexual indiscretion he'd regretted his whole life. The resulting pregnancy had required that honour be fulfilled but the marriage had been doomed. Twelve years of miscarriages had finally resulted in Hugo. His mother had died five years later giving birth to another son who'd died within the week.

Hugo turned away with a sigh.

His father was keeping him waiting for effect. He wanted to rattle Hugo so he'd have the advantage.

Footsteps sounded in the corridor. Loud and intimidating, as they were intended to be. Hugo squared his shoulders and positioned himself with his back to the fireplace as the door opened. The room was cold but the warmth from the flames would provide some meagre bolstering, he hoped.

"Your trunks have gone ahead of you, boy?"

It was the kind of greeting he'd have expected having not seen his father for three months. The scathing correspondence had become a torrent, but his father was more economical in speech.

Hugo nodded. "They have."

"And what do you have to say for yourself."

"I was a fool."

"A fool to squander the inheritance your great aunt kept in trust, enabling you, these past two years, to enjoy a freedom most young men can only dream of."

"It was not much but I was glad not to have to call on you, Father."

"But now I'm the one who has to get you out of this mess of your making."

"If sending me to India is what you mean by that, then yes. I, as you well know, would prefer to remain in London and make my own way in the world until I come into my inheritance in two years."

"So you can marry your little whore? I don't think so."

Hugo steeled himself to remain impassive. His father would goad and goad until he forced the passionate response he was after. He'd done it so many times before, but Hugo was older and wiser now. Charity had helped him see that biting back was futile. And although he despised himself for not defending her good name right now, he felt sure she'd be the first to counsel him against rash words.

Just the thought of what he'd condemned her to was enough to make his knees buckle and his mind whirl with shame.

Though, strangely, it seemed the skills and fortitude Hugo had reluctantly acquired were proving their value. He wasn't shaking like the seven-year-old who'd wept when his father had beaten him. Or his nanny, for that matter. Her swing was, if anything, even more deadly, and Hugo hadn't mourned her for a moment when she'd dropped dead in front of him on his eleventh birthday.

The first time any woman — or man, for that matter — had shown him tenderness was when his father had shoved him into a bedroom at Madame Chambon's and he'd found himself face to face with a trembling, equally terrified, girl.

Now, there was a thought to bolster him.

In the nearly two years since he'd met Charity, Hugo's life had become something he could bear. Something that gave him pleasure, in fact.

He swallowed past the lump in his throat. Now he'd ruined it as effectively as if he'd blown it up with gunpowder.

"You've done your best by me, Father, and I know you want me to show the gratitude you feel is your due. But I have no gratitude when my hand is forced. I do not want to leave England."

"But fools who lose at the gaming table deserve no sympathy, and I am doing what any concerned parent would do who only desires their son to become a man and not throw away his future." Thomas Adams's moustache twitched. He moved towards a cluster of chairs but neither sat nor invited his son to sit. This interview would be over within a couple of minutes. And, within the week, Hugo would be on a boat for far distant shores and his father would be shooting grouse at his country estate.

"Cyril — "

"Made you do it? Come now! You'd blame your cousin for your own actions? That's beyond anything. Disgusting! I can't bear to hear you blather excuses like that. Your cousin is twice the man you'll ever be, and I only wish he were my son."

"He'll be a willing pupil if I should perish and he finally becomes what he and you have always wanted — your heir."

"What rot! Blood will out, and I still have hope that you will become a man I can be proud of. Just because Cyril was with you when you dropped a fortune is of no account to me."

Hugo knew better than to ask his father if he'd put Cyril up to it. His father would have no compunction in using a left hook to defend his dubious practises and Hugo did not want Charity's last sight of him to be in the guise of the victim with a bloodied nose.

At least let him face her with what dignity he could.

"Nothing to say for yourself, as usual?"

Hugo shrugged. It was safer to remain silent when his father was in this mood. He concentrated on the clock on the mantelpiece rather than his father's face, though he could tell by the air of tense anticipation that his father was spoiling for a fight and would be disappointed if Hugo didn't bite.

"So, that's it then." The older man looked disappointed. He rolled his shoulders and balled his fists briefly before adding, "Your uncle will meet you at the docks at dawn the day you leave."

"Then I wish you all the best, father," Hugo said without warmth though nearly lightheaded with relief that this interview was over as he took a step towards the door.

"You can save your farewells for I shall be on the quay, also." His father stopped him with a mirthless laugh. "No need to look surprised. I'm doing my due diligence to ensure you don't bring your little harlot on board. The captain has also been given orders to keep an eye out for stowaways."

Hugo clenched his teeth and turned. "Her name is Charity and she is the most decent and honest woman I have ever met," he muttered.

"Well, I'm sure she knows better than to knock at my door asking for *my* charity when you're gone." His father laughed as if he'd made the greatest joke.

Hugo waited for his mirth to subside. "Charity is the proudest woman I've met. She'd rather die than beg."

"Shows how little you know women, my boy," his father said, still seemingly light-hearted from his unusual foray into levity. "A girl's got to eat and you're no longer her meal ticket. She'll be spreading her legs for the next fellow she's already got lined up before your boat has left harbour — "

His sentence was truncated by a cry of outrage rather than pain as Hugo's fist shot out, collecting him on the jaw.

But the response was quicker than Hugo could see coming.

As he knew it would be.

"Puling, pathetic creature," his father taunted, looking down at Hugo lying at his feet. "Wipe that bloody nose and get out of here." With a hefty kick that collected Hugo's rib cage, his father loomed over him, his eyes bulbous over his thick nose and luxuriant moustache. His teeth were bared and his pleasure was genuine for, once again, he could end his latest altercation with his son as the clear victor. "It's a big bad world out there, my boy, and you need to learn that it's deeds and actions that make a man. Not pretty words and paintings."

CHAPTER 3

*H*ugo wove his way through the streets and alleyways, holding his ribcage and trying not to limp, until he was in Soho. He could navigate his way to Madame Chambon's blindfolded if he had to.

And right now, he'd never been more desperate for a pair of tender arms to fall into and a kind word. He didn't deserve any of it, of course, and if he wanted to be truly hard on himself, he'd deny himself even this pleasure — if he didn't know how much Charity also needed whatever comfort he could give her.

She ran down the stairs with a cry of

pleasure when he was announced while the other girls looked on with mixed expressions. He could read the pity and the condemnation in their eyes, but that didn't matter compared with being alone with the only girl he cared about. The only girl he ever *would* care about.

"Hugo, I wasn't sure when I'd see you again!"

"I'll see you every moment I can until I'm dragged away," he muttered, taking her hand and leading her to the stairs. "Come, dearest, there are some matters I need to talk to you about."

"Oh, but Hugo, you're hurt!" She stopped halfway up the stairs, gasping when she saw him wince. "Your cheek is swollen. And why are you holding your side? Who did this to you?"

Her concern and outrage that someone should have harmed him made up for all the other times there'd been no one to dress his cuts or offer him a word of sympathy. Gently he kissed the top of her head before squeezing her hand and indicating that they continue to her room. She didn't need to know how powerless he was in the face of his father's determination that Hugo be removed from her orbit. It might make her lose heart when, even in his darkest hours, he still held out hope that one day, yes, *one day*, they might be reunited when he'd carried out his sentence and regained his freedom.

He wouldn't deserve her if, by some miracle, she was there waiting for him on the docks in two years, but right now it was the only hope he had.

After a long look, Charity forbore to question him, pressing herself close to his uninjured side, as if in silent solidarity with the pain she instinctively knew he was suffering.

Charity didn't need to be told what he was feeling. She was like some angel of goodness sent to earth to give him the strength he needed to navigate each day.

With the door closed behind them, she pointed to the bed, all practicality. "Now, take off your shirt and let me see the bruising. I'll find some liniment." She helped him loosen his clothes, trailing her hand gently down his side.

"Will you tell me who did this to you? And why?" Her voice was infinitely tender.

Hugo shook his head. "It's best I don't, my love."

She didn't press the point. "Come, let me look after you," she said, kneeling on the bed beside him after she'd ordered him to lie on his back.

Hugo closed his eyes and let his mind wander, revelling in her gentle touch and the quiet comfort of her presence as she rubbed in the soothing lotion.

"I love you so much," he whispered.

"I know you do." Rhythmically, she massaged his chest, avoiding pressure on his injured side. "And you mustn't despair, Hugo."

Hugo felt the lump in his throat grow. How could he not despair? His actions had ramifications that could destroy the angel beside him. How could he have been such a fool as to take the bait Cyril had offered? He'd never trusted his cousin when they were children so why had he accepted that fatal final whiskey and that ridiculous challenge? First Hugo had lost to Cyril, then Cyril had suggested he could win back, not only what he'd lost, but a vast sum more from another bosky fellow who clearly had been in on the ruse.

He clenched his fists and fought the tears — and the little voice always perched on his shoulder that parroted the poison his father had spouted his whole life: *you're worthless, you're a fool. You deserve nothing!*

He *was* a fool and he certainly didn't deserve Charity. But allowing himself to be defeated so easily was hardly going to save Charity from the sordid life to which he'd condemned her if he didn't do something to rectify the situation.

Sitting up abruptly, he put his hands on her shoulders and looked into her eyes. Blue and beautiful and pools of innocence. She *was* innocent and he'd give his life to keep her as safe and protected as she was in this moment.

Right now, she had him to pay the bills that would keep her benefactress satisfied, and a roof over her head and food on the table. He paid for her clothes and any other necessities and entertainments. It was a modest life but at least it meant she didn't have to take on other clients. And it seemed to satisfy Madame Chambon.

"I sold a painting this morning. It didn't fetch much." No need to know that Lord Cowdril had haggled Hugo down to half his asking price after he'd voiced appreciation having seen the picture by chance when he'd stopped Hugo in the street. Hugo had been on his way to give it to Charity. "Also, a couple of pieces of my mother's jewellery and my boxing gloves and fencing equipment. It's very little but it'll buy you a couple of weeks." His heart was pumping. It all sounded so inadequate. What were two weeks when he needed to cover one hundred and three? That was how many remained until his twenty-fifth birthday when he'd come into his grandfather's inheritance. "I've spoken to Madame Chambon and she's promised to continue to house you provided I keep the funds coming."

Charity stroked his cheek. "You're sweet. The girls are very jealous of me, you know." Her smile was gentle. She was trying so hard to make this easy for him. Yet he knew how terrified she must be feeling inside. He had to make sure she knew he'd not let her down. That he'd send her whatever he could.

"Jealous? That you've allied yourself with a good-for-nothing who loses his entire fortune at the gaming table so he can't follow through on his promises?"

Charity shrugged, then leaned into him, drawing his head against her breast and stroking his cheek. "What other gentleman here visits with anything else on their minds other than their own self-gratification?"

"I swear you will never become one of Madame Chambon's girls! You're my girl and I'll find some way to look after you until we can marry." He closed his eyes and breathed in the sweet scent of her freshly bathed skin. She was intoxicating. "When I sail you will lose my protection here," he whispered.

She was silent a long time, digesting his words. She knew how much he wanted her.

Needed her. "Perhaps I could join you, later?"

It was painful to answer. "Don't think I've not gone over every such possibility but..." He shook his head, shifting so he could look at her. "There's a reason none of the other fellows take wives until they're thirty. One needs to be in a decent financial position and able to settle down somewhere that's safe for a wife and family. The conditions are intolerable. The heat, malaria... Diseases like cholera and dysentery are rife. It's no place for a woman, or so I've been told by anyone who's experienced it."

The lamp flickered and Hugo stared at the red flock wallpaper as his mind did its ever-revolving circuit of drawing in one possibility or another, only to discard each one. "My father will keep me on short rations, while my uncle will be ever vigilant. Father is determined I marry whom he deems a respectable wife."

Charity let out a short laugh. Hugo could not believe her restraint in letting him off the hook when she could have wept and thrown things at him for ruining what they had and for destroying their future together.

No, *jeopardising* their future together. He would be back. He had to believe he'd not die of jungle fever before he'd returned to London to save Charity.

"The irony, my darling," she went on, almost as if she were at a tea party and discussing some amusing *on-dit*. "If my respectable papa had honoured his promise to marry my once-respectable late mama, I'd have been the legitimate daughter of a viscount."

The irony had often struck Hugo, too.

"Sadly, there are many of us by-blows in similar positions to me," she went on, indicating her sordid surroundings, her voice lighter than it ought to have been, considering the sorry truth of it. "It's all too easy for an entitled gentleman to have a bit of fun with the staff. He wouldn't dream of marrying one of them, though." She shrugged. "Or acknowledging a bastard. It's just not the done thing, my darling."

Hugo looked her in the eye. She rarely spoke about her father but a sudden hope had taken root. "Do you know who your father is? Where he is?"

Charity's smile was indulgent. "Yes. But I'm not going to approach him, if that's what you're implying. Mama tried that and the distress of his dismissal nearly undid her. He questioned whether I was his. He'll hardly say any different, now, more than ten years later."

Hugo hung his head, then, on a swift thought, dropped his hand to her belly. "You couldn't possibly be — ?"

"I'm not," she reassured him. "Madame makes certain her girls know how to protect themselves from at least that inconvenience."

"Lord, Charity, all I want to do is marry you and have children with you."

"And paint and write poems."

"Yes, but it's only because of you that I can do that. Thinking of you unleashes something inside me that makes me feel intoxicated with possibility."

"Then think of me when you're gone, and send me those pictures and poems, because that's what's going to sustain *me* while you're off hunting tigers and picking tea leaves, and laying railway tracks, my darling Hugo." She drew him down beside her and snuggled into his warmth.

Visually tracing the pressed metal ceiling with his gaze while he thought of how he might incorporate it in a sketch, he said, "I've brought you a painting and a poem I've been working on all week. *Christmas Charity* it's called. Or *Christmas Wedding*, I can't decide which."

"I'll treasure both," she said, reaching up to stroke his face. "But please don't think of me as a charity case. Between us, we *will* find a way to grasp the future we thought we had."

SHE DIDN'T BELIEVE IT BUT HUGO NEEDED TO hear it. And as he kissed her, Charity tried to stop herself from wondering how many more times she'd feel the touch of his lips.

But she was determined to be brave.

"Please don't go," she begged when he rolled off her and sat up. "We don't have much time. I want to make the most of every minute."

He smiled, his mouth turned up but his eyes grim as he whipped back the covers and kissed the two rosy buds on her breasts, then her belly button and, finally, the mound at the juncture of her legs.

"As do I but my main priority right now is ensuring that you are safe when I'm gone. By God, if I could marry you this moment and not negate my claim to everything that will one day be both of ours, I would." For a moment he was quiet as he stood over her. "Charity, do you resent me for not whisking you down the aisle? That is, if we had enough time for the banns to be read before I sailed?"

She drew the covers up to her chin and averted her eyes. A small part of her did. "I'd marry you if you were a prince or a pauper," she whispered, instead.

"But if I marry you now, I will forever *be* a pauper. We truly would have nothing. My father would pull every string he had to en-sure we suffered in perpetuity. I'd have nothing to offer you."

He leaned over and kissed her lips with even greater tenderness. "Believe me, Charity, if we can survive the next two years, our future is secure. I want to be able to sail back into Southampton to claim my inheritance and marry you in a public ceremony full of pomp and circumstance." He reached for something and straightened, branding a piece of parchment. "Here's my poem. Read it when I'm gone. You think I'm capable only of daydreams but I will prove to you that where I am motivated by my muse, I am capable of anything. Now I really do have to leave, my precious. There are still some people I must see in the hopes of finding some respectable employment for you that I can supplement with the wages I shall send you while I'm away."

CHARITY TRIED TO BE HEARTENED BY Hugo's poem but it only made her cry even harder. How could he imagine a society wedding, with a church filled with guests truly wishing them both the greatest happiness, could ever be their destiny? How could he imagine these same people would be smiling and tossing rose petals at them as Charity and Hugo stepped into a carriage and were borne away into the sunset, towards the estate that would one day be Hugo's — if he remained unmarried until his twenty-fifth birthday?

Hugo was the sweetest, kindest, most honourable man Charity knew but he was a dreamer.

And so was Charity if she thought there could be a happy ending to their tragic love story.

AND NOW IT WAS HER DEAR FRIEND'S wedding.

In Violet's small first-floor bedchamber, Charity stared at the girl who'd been so kind to her, a vision in bridal white as the two of them stood before the mirror.

Normal young women in such a setting would have hearts full of joy.

But they were not normal young women and this was not a normal situation.

Violet smiled sadly. She must have seen the tears gathering in Charity's eyes for she turned to pat her shoulder and whisper, "There now, it's not a happy ending for me, either. But this is today. Think what could happen tomorrow."

Violet was always so sanguine about life. Sanguine yet optimistic enough to believe that tomorrow *could* be better.

Charity touched the exquisite lace veil that partly obscured her friend's beautiful face. "You have so much more to complain about than I. Yet tonight will be your greatest sorrow for having to acknowledge that your wedding is a lie."

"He'd marry me if he could — just as Hugo would marry you. Now, come." Violet held out her hand and together they went out into the cold night air where a hackney was waiting to convey them to the church.

Charity's role as a witness — a charade — was a revelation. She was unused to being out in the real world amongst society people. To see the genuine tears of joy wet the cheeks of the elderly aunt of the man Violet was pretending to marry gave her a small measure of pleasure.

Lord Belvedere, Violet's intended who was waiting at the altar, also looked surprisingly in love considering this was a sham marriage to please his dying aunt who desired to see him wed above all else. Innocent Miss Thistlethwaite had no idea who Violet was. Or, more to the point, *what* Violet really was. She thought her a shop girl yet still she was pleased she was marrying her nephew. Which meant that she thought Charity was a shop girl, too, and yet she was happy enough to say to her, as if they were on an equal footing, "When a girl is as lovely as dear Violet, she can do no wrong." Then, disconcertingly, she'd asked, as they took their places in church, "And where do you hail from, my dear? Who are your people?"

A reckless gambler? A lowly governess? Charity had not known what to say for one hardly admitted to being the illegitimate offspring of such a mismatched union.

So, she merely lowered her eyes and said demurely, "No one you'd know, ma'am."

"Come now, my dear. We cannot choose the station into which we are born. And honest toil is always to be commended for that is what this nation has been built upon."

Emboldened, partly by the woman's kindness and partly by her own long-held resentment, Charity replied, "My mother was a good and honest woman but my father was not so prudent."

And now Charity's only chance of happiness was again to be foiled by excess and vice; the lure of chance at a gambling table.

Miss Thistlethwaite who could not have known the details of Hugo's ruin and banishment, said, with a shake of her head, "Reckless young men are too rarely called upon to account for the havoc they cause."

And then she was turning towards the priest, silent and expectant, while her words resonated in Charity's head.

Who was the reckless young man in all this? It wasn't only Hugo. It was his slippery cousin who had enticed Hugo as if his main purpose was to ruin him.

Charity recalled what the other girls had

said about him and his reputation. Clearly, she wasn't the only one who thought Mr Adams needed to be called to account.

A deep hush had fallen over the sparse congregation as bride and groom stood before the man who, to all intents and purposes, was officiating over their shared future.

What a terrible sham this all was, and all because some entitled gentleman thought he could run roughshod over the happiness of those more vulnerable than themselves.

At least Violet's handsome Lord Belvedere had been honest from the outset. The first night he'd met Violet, in fact.

Cyril had simply resorted to slippery deeds to achieve his aims.

Well, he would not succeed.

Even at this late stage, when common sense told Charity that it was far too late to change their destinies, she felt the anger within like a flaming torch.

Charity had always been sweet and passive.

And look where that had got her poor, dead, disgraced mother?

Watching Violet intone her vows in a voice that was pure and charged with emotion, Charity decided the time had come when no risk was too great. If Hugo was not able to marry, support or even be with Charity, then what did Charity have to lose.

Surely there was some way of proving Mr Adams the cheat he was?

And, in doing so, maybe — just, maybe — she could save them both.

CHAPTER 4

$\mathcal{O}$nly three more days. Shivering in her thin dressing gown, Charity marked off the calendar on her wall then went to sit on her bed to think.

It was late morning and she could hear a little movement in the house. The chink of buckets wielded by the servants and muted conversation from several of the other girls who were in the passageway.

She heard Rosetta protest something too loudly, as was her wont, and, on impulse, Charity threw open the door of her bedchamber to call after them. Time was running out and she was panicking.

"I need to help Hugo," she said without

preamble. She knew she must look as desperate as she felt. She'd thought she and Hugo might try and come up with a plan together, but Charity feared Hugo didn't have enough aggression and fire within him to counteract the evil Cyril, when, after a night of deep contemplation, she'd decided that was what was needed.

Emily sat on the bed. "I know he's a regular at a gambling den called The Red Door."

"And," said Emily, "my Thursday gentleman, Mr Mortimer, is willing to let us in, as long as we're discreet. Yes, you asked for our help, but we're ahead of you, Charity."

"We thought you'd be too naïve to know where to start," said Rosetta, examining her fingernails. She glanced at her friend, then said in a rush. "All of us girls have been discussing it. We don't want you to have to earn your living like the rest of us. That's why we're discovering everything we can so that — " she shrugged — "you'll avoid our terrible fate." Her tone was harsh but Charity recognised the sentiment behind them and tears stung her eyes. These women had been forced into the kind of work Charity was terrified of and appalled by but they still had enough goodness in their hearts to try and protect her from it.

She clasped her hands together. "Thank you," she said softly. "For both your sakes, I will try and be less naive and — " she cleared her throat — "more underhand and devious for I do appreciate all the effort you're going to."

"I think you shouldn't try to be under-hand and devious unless it's specifically under our direction," said Emily hastily with a meaningful look at Rosetta. "We've had lots of practise and there's nothing that can ruin a plan so quickly as a novice with good intentions."

"Then what should I do?" asked Charity, relieved of course that she'd been let off the hook — to a certain extent, at any rate.

"Come to the Red Door with us on Thursday."

Charity nodded. A great weight seemed to fall from her shoulders. It was all very well to decide that Mr Cyril Adams should be called to account but, in truth, she'd not had the first idea as to how she could go about it.

Rosetta and Emily, however, were well versed in the ways of this treacherous world.

The fact that they were so motivated to help her made her realise that, with such friends, somehow, Charity would survive.

THE RED SATIN GOWN WAS LAVISHLY ornamented with bows and sparkles while the feathers in Charity's hair were the perfect complement.

She looked just as she was supposed to. As, she supposed, everyone imagined her to be: a harlot. A lightskirt. A barque of frailty, a lightskirt, en *horizontale*. As such, the attention she garnered was not surprising. Gentlemen leered at her through their monocles as she sashayed, in Rosetta and Emily's wake, into the tobacco-filled air of one of the most insalubrious residences of Soho.

But her palms were sweating inside her

elbow-length gloves and she could feel the sheen of it on her carefully applied makeup.

Emily had worked wonders on her face so that she almost didn't look like herself. Actually, she rather liked the way she looked though she was glad her mother would never see her.

Glad her mother had never lived to see her only child become what she had worked so hard to try to prevent. But, really, that was always rather a vain hope for, without a father who would recognise her, and with no money and no references, what chance had Charity of being anything else?

"There he is!" Rosetta's excited whisper was augmented with a sharp tug of her skirt and Charity glanced up to follow the direction in which she was pointing.

She'd not seen Hugo's cousin, Mr Cyril Adams, before. The gentleman had only been described to her as a mischief-maker, an untrustworthy type. So very unlike Hugo.

The fact that she'd sent a note to Hugo asking him to come here was the only reason Charity didn't crumple up in a heap just to see Hugo's nemesis. *Their* nemesis.

Mr Adams was about the same age as Hugo and, from this distance, there was a similarity in visage — the square shape of the jaw — but whereas Hugo's was moulded in a way that made him appear always pleasant-natured, Mr Adams', when combined with the sharpness of his expression and the glittering intensity of his eyes, made him seem like a man determined to get what he wanted.

Charity tried not to look at him too pointedly. Was she just imagining this, knowing what Mr Adams had done to her darling Hugo? He'd ruined his own cousin, no doubt to further his own ends. Hugo had said even before all this terribleness, that his father favoured his nephew over his own son and had said in as many words that he preferred a man of action over a poet.

"What if he realises who I am?" she asked in sudden panic as Mr Adams glanced in their direction.

"He won't and that's why this plan is such a good one." Rosetta smiled at her, confident for once. Smug, even. "We have two avenues for seeking success."

"Two?" Charity had only heard of the first. Her heart did a skittering dance in her chest and didn't settle down. At the far end of an enormous billiards table, a tall, broad-shouldered gentleman was flanked by a couple of laughing fellows who seemed to be leering at every woman who entered the room. Like they were sport.

A game of roulette was taking place in one corner and several card tables were occupied by some characters with their heads bent low over their hands.

Charity didn't know the first thing about how to play the games of chance that were the lifeblood of this place.

She gripped Emily's lace-edged sleeve. "Will I be expected to play?"

Emily shook her head. "No. I might, though. I'm considered rather a dab hand. Rosetta has a keen pair of eyes and she'll be doing her best to catch him in the act."

"You think you will?" Charity put her hand to her chest. Her heart was beating so painfully she thought it would burst out of her bodice.

"No." Emily's response was matter-of-fact. "That's why we think we'll have to work with our second plan."

"And what's that? Why didn't you tell me?" Charity had done everything they'd asked with such blind obedience but now she realised she'd not questioned them at all.

"Our second plan involves going with him to his room where you'll hopefully find a list of gentlemen our delightful Mr Cyril Adams is currently blackmailing. Or rather, find the reasons he has dredged up in order to make his little ploy so successful."

"What? *Me*?" Charity nearly choked on the word. "How can I possibly do that? I mean, I can't."

Rosetta, who had been conversing with a gentleman a little distance away, now turned back, slipping into position next to Emily.

"We rather thought you might protest if we told you. But really, Charity, you're the only one who will have any chance of doing this. He doesn't know you at all, you're very sweet and innocent, and so you're the last person he'd suspect if you go with him to his room."

"To his room? Why would he even ask me? And if he does, what if he tries to...?"

She saw the other two girls exchange smiles. With a faint shrug of her shoulders, Rosetta said, "If Hugo doesn't win back his fortune, you're going to lose him forever. And you're going to have to hike your skirts and spread your legs for any gentleman who desires it at Madame Chambon's." She encompassed the room with a sweep of her arm. "Any gentleman here, for that matter. We don't want that, as we've told you. But surely the risk of doing this *just once* with Mr Adams is worth it?"

Charity felt her insides shrivel. She closed her eyes as Rosetta went on, "However, if you succeed in finding what you're looking for, Emily and I have secured promises of enormous gratitude from various of our regulars while it will also ensure your Hugo is vindicated."

Charity put her hand to her mouth, then

quickly altered her expression knowing of course that her shock and horror would only draw attention to them. Forcing herself to look natural, she whispered, "You brought me here to find out what your gentlemen wanted to know? Not to help Hugo?" She'd thought them her friends. Believed they were acting only in her best interests.

Emily grasped her shoulder as she turned away. Drawing her into the shadows of a fringed, red velvet curtain, she spoke as if to an errant child. "We set about discovering how we might protect you from what you see as a fate worse than death, Charity. And if the waters have been muddied, don't blame us."

The expression on her normally sweet, placid face, was fierce. "Rosetta and I have been exploring myriad ways we might bring down Mr Adams in order to vindicate your Hugo." She bit her lip, appeared to hesitate, then ploughed on. "Each evening, when the gentlemen arrive downstairs to choose who to while away a few hours of their time with, we have accepted only those whom we believe might have some useful knowledge of Mr Adams." Her fingers dug into Charity's shoulder as she emphasised her point. "Because information is the only currency that can benefit any of us. And the best we could come up with is that your Mr Adams is a cheat but a clever, slippery cheat who has never been caught." She sighed. "And is unlikely to be caught tonight. But he is suspected of dabbling in blackmail and that is what is of most interest to our gentlemen." She indicated Mr Adams across the room with a furtive look. He was in conversation now with a couple of other gentlemen, one elderly, one young, neither of them the fast set as far as Charity could tell, if their attire and demeanour was anything to go by.

The Red Door was a gaming hellhole but even respectable members of society came here.

"The elder gentleman is Mr Russell. He enjoyed my favours two nights ago though he will not acknowledge me in public, naturally. He fears that information that would compromise his son and possibly destroy his political ambitions *may* be in the hands of Mr Adams. And he's prepared to pay a great deal to ensure this does not happen."

"But this is all…impossible to ascertain. I cannot do so, surely? Where would I even begin to look? And with him wide awake having…having had his way with me?" Charity blinked back tears. She had to be stronger than this. But she was not going to sacrifice herself for such dubious gains.

Nervously she glanced over her shoulder. "I'd make a mull of it. I'm not clever like you," she added to Rosetta who had just returned to the conversation.

"Mr Adams would be far too suspicious of us," said Rosetta. "However, you, who have never been seen at Madame Chambon's or anywhere else for that matter, would make the perfect candidate."

"He already has me in his sights." Charity felt a surge of panic at the memory. "You heard Madame Chambon saying he was asking for me the night after Hugo lost to him. He wanted to exact an even greater revenge on Hugo."

"But he has no idea what Hugo's beloved

looks like. I agree, if he did, he'd be suspicious of your motives. But you are an ingenue. Do you see the way the gentlemen are looking at you? They're intrigued. They've never seen you grace the velvet sofas of Madame Chambon's where they seek diversion. You're young and full of grace and Mr Adams, from the way his gaze keeps darting in this direction, would be most amenable to a little show of interest from you."

With a pat on her shoulder, Rosetta pushed Charity forward.

"I've had no practise in what I should do. I'll ruin everything." Charity knew she looked as panicked as she felt.

"It's your obvious lack of experience that will win the day, Charity," said Emily. "Madame Chambon believes it and you're one of her favourites. She actually wants you to win your happily ever after with your beloved Hugo." She pursed her lips and exchanged a wry look with Rosetta. "She said it would be a feather in her cap to promote a real wedding in view of Violet's disappointment."

"You've been discussing it with Madame Chambon?"

"And the other girls. We thought it would be best to bring you here without the benefit of the information we've just imparted to you." Rosetta smiled comfortably.

"Hugo will help me," Charity muttered under her voice and with a defiant look. "He knows I'm coming here tonight and he won't let anything bad happen to me."

Rosetta rolled her eyes. "We left a note at Madame's to say you were elsewhere. Please don't look so upset but he had the potential to ruin everything."

Charity stared up at the two girls and then at the swarming, terrifying room before her. She caught an interested look or two from some of the male contingent and quickly looked away as heat burned her cheeks.

In a few days Hugo was sailing away. She knew that when he finally disappeared out of sight it might well be the last time she'd ever see him again. And for all his fevered attempts at securing her future, the money and promises he'd put in place would not last for long.

What choice did she have? She simply had to take her chances tonight.

"You might need this, Charity." Rosetta dug in her reticule and handed what Charity at first thought to be a lace handkerchief before she felt something hard beneath.

"Put it straight into your pocket and only use it if occasion demands," her friend said, lowering her voice and appearing to remove a piece of lint from her shoulder as she moved her head closer. "It's a pair of dice, loaded to favour a four and a five. As I said, Emily and I will be handling the gambling, if called upon but, in a place like this, one never knows what might happen. Nor would anyone believe someone as sweet and innocent looking as you capable of underhand tactics."

Charity stared about the room, mostly populated by men so that she and the few other finely dressed women stood out as the *demimondaine*.

In the dim light, they seemed to move in

and out of focus; one moment dressed in dark suits, the next in wolf's clothing.

Indeed, they *were* wolves who would converge on her when she was without a protector. The accusations of childlike innocence with which Emily and Rosetta charged her were true. Her guileless mother had taught her nothing of life. Not that Charity had spent much time with her mother since she'd worked for as long as she could remember to look after her mother's imbecile older sister. That had, she supposed, been some small use for an illegitimate child who could not be acknowledged by the family. And, after that aunt had died — without ever having addressed Charity by name — Charity had found herself on a coach to London, to make her own way in the world following her mother's funeral.

The only people who had ever been kind to her were Madame Chambon and the girls.

And Hugo.

She bowed her head for a second, then brought up her chin. "So tonight will be a test of my abilities. I have no idea what will be required of me and I'm certain I won't succeed in ferreting out any useful information. But if I can help Hugo in any small way, and ensure that his own future is not blighted forever, I will."

"Oh, look," said Emily, pointing. "Mr Adams is coming this way."

CHAPTER 5

The knowledge of how much he needed to achieve in such a short time hung heavily on Hugo's shoulders as he turned his footsteps towards Soho.

At any other time, he would have stopped to wonder at the miracle wrought by a blanketing of pristine snow upon a poor neighbourhood, turning it into a wonderland of beauty and promise.

He might have felt uplifted by the carollers on the street corner praising the Lord their Saviour in pure, joyful voices.

But the familiar words of *God Rest Ye Merry Gentlemen* brought pain not comfort to Hugo's ears as he bowed his head and trudged past them.

Fear not, then said the angel,
Let nothing you affright,
This day is born a Savior,
Of virtue, power, and might;

Hugo was all too aware that he should have been able to comfort Charity with such sentiments, reassuring her that he would be her saviour, a man of virtue, power, and might.

Instead, he was going to have to explain to her that the best he'd managed was to find her a position as a photographer's assistant. And then, suspicious of the man's motives in wanting a young and pretty assistant, he'd turned down the job offer.

It seemed that every moment since his disastrous evening with Cyril he'd been on the back foot trying to salvage something from the wreckage of his life.

He'd tried so hard to find some respectable employment that would make it easier for Charity to be accepted as his wife upon his twenty-fifth birthday but it seemed word had got around. No family member or friend of any female relative had need of a companion let alone a governess. It was as if they all knew his little secret and had closed ranks against him.

Nearby, a ladder-man was pasting advertisements to a hoarding. Pausing to cross the road, Hugo looked up at the posters of electric corsets and others advertising miracle cures for chilblains and scrofula. The young woman with her hour-glass figure proclaiming the healthful effects of her combinations reminded him of Charity with her long, chestnut tresses and peaches and cream complexion and he was struck by the most intense desire to run all the way to the dreadful house where she lived and commit to memory the feel of her curves as he buried his face in her fragrant hair.

Not that he deserved this, though he liked to think she would draw some comfort from his assurances that he'd die rather than see her forced into prostitution to keep body and soul together.

He dug in his pocket and withdrew the painting he'd worked on since he'd sketched her so hastily as she lay sleeping just before he'd left her. He wanted to study it in the natural light for he'd been somewhat feverish as he'd worked at his masterpiece in the semi-darkness.

He touched the tendrils of hair at her temples. If only he had his paintbrush with him now, he could render the soft curls a little more perfectly.

He unfolded the picture and held it up. It was, perhaps, one of his finest works, despite the fact that in real life her hair was more lustrous than he'd rendered it.

And her eyes were much more arresting than he'd managed, though he wasn't displeased with the finished piece.

However, all pleasure evaporated at the reminder that he was giving her this because of their impending separation. He'd done numerous drawings of her this past week, wanting to commit her image to his memory but wanting, also, to ensure she'd be in no doubt as to how important she was to him.

A sudden gust of wind whipped the drawing out of his fingers and he tried to snatch it before it caught an eddying breeze that lifted it, fluttering airborne for a moment, before arriving level with the ladder man.

"I say!" Looking down from his precarious position, the ladder man snatched at Hugo's work of art, turning to look at him with a grin. "Nice young lady like this ought to be admired by the world!" he declared cheerfully as he pasted the back with glue then slapped the drawing over the single gap on the busy hoarding.

"You can't do that!" Hugo protested but the ladder man ignored him as he sloshed his glue-laden paintbrush over the front for good measure.

"Not going to see your young lady this evening, then?"

Hugo, about to protest further, turned to see Lord Belvedere on the other side of the road. The fellow looked as if he hadn't a care in the world and Hugo tried to push aside his real thoughts as he nodded in greeting. Belvedere was off to foreign lands, adventuring by choice, leaving behind Charity's friend, Violet. Life was easier if one had no scruples, he supposed, though he liked Belvedere, nonetheless.

"I'm going there now," he said, crossing the road.

"You won't find her at home." Lord Belvedere had resumed walking but he said over his shoulder, "Got to dash. But anyway, I saw her just now at the Red Door."

Hugo watched Belvedere disappear around a corner while he tried to assimilate what Charity would be doing in such a den of iniquity. Nothing safe, he feared, and wondered if her friends had persuaded her to go there with them.

His anxiety increased as he made his way to the notorious gambling den.

Cyril frequented places like this.

But not Charity. Why would she go there unless she'd got it into her head to take matters into her own hands? To try to beat Cyril at his own game?

Charity knew nothing of places like this. For all that she lived in a brothel, she was remarkably sheltered.

He hastened his stride.

Taking on Cyril meant Charity would be

throwing herself into the path of a man without compassion or morals. He'd eat Charity for lunch and spit her out, if only to spite Hugo. Cyril was a bounder, a cheat, a reprobate. Ever since they'd been children they'd been at war. If Cyril wanted anything to do with Charity, it was only so he could use her as the ultimate revenge against Hugo.

He wiped the back of his hand across his sweating forehead as his breath hitched.

"Are you all right, sir?"

Hugo stopped, blinking at the elderly woman passing by on the pavement on her husband's arm.

"Quite alright, thank you," he said, nodding his thanks and resisting the urge to break into an unseemly run.

The Red Door. He knew where to find it though he'd never been there. He certainly had no desire to go there, now, but if Charity was inside and putting herself in danger, he had no choice.

The cobblestones were slippery as he turned into a narrow alley. The snow had turned to slush and there was nothing

magical about this part of the neighbourhood.

Hugo forced himself to stop and take
stock. He couldn't burst inside without a
plan. If Charity was at the gaming table,
hoping to effect some miracle means of re-
versing the damage Hugo had wrought then
the very least Hugo could do was find a
means of safeguarding her from his evil
cousin — using his brains rather than wild
impulse.

Yes, Cyril was evil.

The Red Door was a gambling den and
Cyril was a gambler. A gambler, swindler,
and cheat.

And how did one defeat a cheat?

Beneath the overhang of a crooked dou-
ble-storied dwelling in an insalubrious al-
leyway, he stopped to consider the question,
startling as a mangy cat rubbed against his
ankle.

Cheats were sly and secretive. They
caught one by surprise, just as Cyril had
done when he'd plied Hugo with drink and
then challenged him, on his sweetheart's
honour, to a game of Hazard.

What did cheats resort to? They resorted to cheating, of course.

A terrible thought struck Hugo; one that he would never have entertained had he not been desperate.

A short diversion was all that was required for him to equip himself with the tools that he hoped might be at least of some help to getting his darling Charity out of the terrible situation he'd created.

CHAPTER 6

*C*harity ran her tongue over her top lip and fanned herself as she smiled at the gentleman facing her across the gaming table. Despite the snow outside, it was hot upstairs with the multitude of bodies pressed up against one another as they gambled, drank, and flirted with the few women about.

The smoke from the cheroots the gentlemen smoked made the back of her throat feel scratchy but, of course, she had to smile and pretend she was in her element. Ladies had to *always* pretend they were enjoying themselves.

Mr Cyril Adams, it appeared, was definitely out to enjoy a night on the town. He was dressed in the latest fashion, his coat well cut with contrasting collar, his waistcoat decorated with a watch chain and a diamond pin adorning his Ascot tie.

Yes, he might look the part but Charity wondered how well accepted he was by society in general when rumour described the ways he'd earned his pile of coin. Their grandfather had earned a fortune through honest trade, half of which Mr Cyril was to inherit, but in the meantime, he'd earned his own dubious fortune—which ebbed and flowed, she'd heard.

Mr Adams now leant over the table to give Charity a more assessing look. "What's your name, lovely lady?"

Charity had been preparing herself but it was nevertheless a shock to find herself face to face with Hugo's nemesis — and hers.

For here was Cyril Adams close up. Ever since her friends had whispered excitedly that this was the gentleman she was to impress, she'd been watching him covertly.

He certainly fancied himself as a ladies' man, the way he'd tossed his head as he'd swaggered up to the baize-topped table that was littered with markers, coins, and banknotes.

"I've not seen you before. What's your name, lovely lady and are you going to make me a lucky man this evening?" he asked.

Charity dropped her gaze and blushed easily. "My name's Cathie," she murmured. She was not about to step into any trap by revealing her true identity. "And I don't think I'm your lucky charm because I've never gambled before."

"Then you'll be worth your weight in gold for beginner's luck," he said with too much bonhomie. He'd been drinking. She could smell the whisky on his breath as he came around to put his hand on her shoulder and rub his nose against her neck.

Charity tried not to recoil from the brush of his bristly moustache. The next few minutes could make all the difference to how she managed the outcome Emily and Rosetta had worked so hard to mastermind.

Charity must rise to the challenge. She'd

never had a hand in changing her fate — it had always been thrust upon her. But coming here tonight was the first step towards changing what might otherwise be a soul-destroying destiny.

"Oh, sir, but you'll be cross if beginner's luck deserts me," she said, playing upon her innocence.

"A roll of the dice requires nothing in the way of expertise." He seized her hand and pressed something into the palm which she opened, looking rather stupidly at the two white cubes.

"Give me nine and make me a happy man," he said.

Charity glanced around her and realised a few more interested gentlemen had wandered up to the table. Young and middle-aged, there was speculation and definite admiration in the way they sized her up. Even Charity, self-effacing though she was, could see it. It terrified her.

"But the highest number is six," she said, wishing her voice sounded stronger. She pressed her hand against her hip and felt the outline of the two dice in her pocket that

Rosetta had given her. What use would they be to her?

A rumble of genial laughter echoed round the table before Mr Adams said, "Indeed it is, my pretty. But a four and a five make nine, as do a six and a three." He raised her hand to the sky and gently traced the outline of her fist as he declared to the others in their orbit, "My pretty talisman will give me a nine, just see if she doesn't."

Charity now realised that Mr Adams did, in fact, have an opponent, a surly northerner it appeared when he grumbled that he'd waited long enough for play to resume.

"Please, do the honours on my behalf, Miss Cathie."

Charity glanced about her, raised her hand and obediently threw the dice. For what could she do?

A small silence preceded the scattering of the cubes which rolled across the green baize table top. The first landed cleanly upon a five while the second dice rolled slowly towards the edge. The whispering of a couple of gentlemen to her left stirred the curls at her temples and sent a shiver through her.

When a cry of surprise rang out, Charity had only just steeled herself for the jubilation of the man for whom she'd evidently won a good deal at the expense of the northerner.

She began to turn away, more than ready to be swallowed up by the crowd. Mr Adams' die had been loaded, surely?

But then Emily was pushing her back to the table, whispering in her ear, "That one was luck, truly it was, Charity, for his opponent supplied the dice."

And then Mr Adams was swinging her into the crook of his arm as he cried, "Gentlemen, my lucky charm! Did I not say she'd win for me?"

But Charity was not going to allow herself to become a plaything with no object other than lining Mr Adams' pockets when Rosetta had a clearer plan in place for later that evening.

Firmly she pushed herself free of his grasp before another opponent had stepped up to the table ready to take on

Hugh's gambling cousin who was, it seemed, more ready for another game of Hazard than following Charity through the throng.

Charity disappeared back into the crowd, her skin still crawling from Mr Adams' touch. She'd utilised every bit of willpower to hide her revulsion for the man who'd actively sought to destroy her beloved Hugo; a man who, furthermore, wanted to rub salt in the wound by pursuing Charity. Only the fact that he did not know her identity had given her the strength to keep her strong. That, and the fact that Charity knew she had to push herself to do, and be, more than she ever had before. She had to help Hugo as much as she could. Not just to save what they had, as a couple, but to prevent him from leaving on a dangerous journey to a land he had no wish to visit, doing work that was anathema to him. Hugo was a poet and an artist, not an adventurer.

He was not in a position to reverse his

ill-fortune but maybe, just maybe, Charity could.

"The Devil's own luck," Rosetta congratulated her when she was safely in the company of her friends and sipping champagne partly concealed by a tasselled velvet curtain beside a tall sash window that looked onto the street.

"Yes, but I don't know how it's going to do me much good," said Charity, dolefully.

"That's because you haven't the slippery instinct for getting ahead that we have, my dear." Emily's eyes danced as she raised her glass to her lips and drank deeply. "We are going to win big at Mr Adams' expense. The fact that you really did throw what he wanted gives us an enormous advantage."

"How? We have no money to gamble with?"

Emily raised one eyebrow and bit her lip as if withholding a great secret. "I've entered into an arrangement with a special friend who knows exactly what we're about. Someone who has his own concerns regarding Mr Adams. A score to settle, if you will."

Charity's mood plummeted even further. "And I am to be the means by which he will settle his score? No, I can't."

She might have rolled the dice and achieved a successful outcome but she was terrified at the thought of what else she might be required to do.

Emily and Rosetta shared a meaningful glance before Emily said, "My friend, who's here tonight, just spoke to me. He saw the interest our not-very-esteemed Mr Cyril Adams has in you. He thinks you may be able to address his concerns when you go back to his townhouse tonight."

"I can't!" Charity gripped her champagne flute against her chest so hurriedly that the front of her gown suffered from the spillage, causing Emily to lean forward and whisper, as she dabbed at the damp spot, "We've discussed this, Charity, and I've also heard it said just now — by no less an authority than Mr Adams' last valet who was summarily dismissed just last week and who has vengeance in his heart to equal yours — that Mr Adams curates a detailed account book of the various misdemeanours occasioned by various society personages. A blackmail diary if you will. My friend is very anxious to know if he features in that book."

"How can I possibly get access to that book if Mr Adams is...with me the whole time?" Charity straightened with sudden determination. "I can't do it! I won't do it! I won't go back to his house and prostitute myself to...to this man. No! I can't do this to Hugo!"

Emily patted Charity on the shoulder. "It would be the noblest sacrifice for Hugo," she said gently. "Of course, you'd do everything you could to avoid *sleeping* with him but if that's what you had to do to — "

"No! Never! I'd rather starve in a gutter. Don't you see? It wouldn't be noble at all!" Charity stared at her two friends. "It would be the greatest disloyalty to Hugo if I slept with the very man who sought to destroy him."

"Well, you'd try not to, obviously, but Hugo would think you the bravest, noblest person in the whole world that you'd take such risks on his behalf," Rosetta said energetically. "Oh, my Lord!" Her tone changed as a look of shock crossed her features.

"What is it?" Charity and Emily cried in unison, craning their heads to see what had discomposed her.

"It's Hugo. I just saw him in the light of the streetlamp below, about to enter the club. He's on his way now." Rosetta glanced about the crowded room, her face ashen even in this light. "He could ruin everything."

Charity took a step away. "I must leave now," she said, wanting desperately to throw herself into Hugo's arms at the same time as wishing desperately she was as far away as possible from the dangerous, detestable Cyril Adams.

"No, no, I'll waylay him and explain why you're here," Emily said hurriedly, grabbing her wrist to stop her as she communicated something quickly with Rosetta. "He'll know it's in nobody's interests for you to be revealed as his mistress."

Charity wished her friends wouldn't use such language. She didn't see herself as Hugo's mistress and nor did he. It was so much more than that. And if not for Cyril Adams...

Her fear hardened to anger and grew. She turned back from the door to look at her beloved's cousin. Son of Satan, that's what he was. Like Hugo, he was descended from the same enterprising steel merchant but he was as different from Hugo as it was possible to be.

Cyril was cut from the same cloth, it seemed, as both his father and his uncle who wanted their cake and to eat it. They wanted to be richer than anyone else, they didn't mind what they did to achieve this — and yet they wanted to be accepted by society.

Well, it wasn't so easy. Charity knew that very well.

Casting a last look at the gaming table where Cyril's floppy dark hair obscured his sneer of concentration, Charity drew back into the crowd. No matter how much she desperately wanted to see Hugo, she must keep away from him. Charity needed to be a much finer actress than she was if she were to hide her dangerously transparent feelings for him from the world.

From Mr Cyril Adams.

"Hurry, Charity! This way!" Rosetta steered her through a knot of guests congregated by the supper table but a tall, sandy-haired gentleman reached out his hand to grip her by the wrist and draw her within the circle of his discussion, saying, "My dear little friend, meet my associate, Mr Daniel Roberts — "

And in that moment, the double doors from the lobby were thrown open and Hugo stood upon the threshold, staring in their direction as if he had a sixth sense telling him exactly where to look for the woman he sought.

Charity couldn't move without making a scene for she was trapped between Rosetta and an elderly gentleman who looked about to speak to her in a very warm fashion as she turned in the hopes of side-stepping Hugo's piercing glance.

But he'd sighted her and was advancing with speed and determination.

"Excuse me, but I must — " She ended

on a whisper, turning only enough to extricate herself from the immediate group before Hugo was pressing against her, albeit briefly as he contoured her waist before plunging his hand into her pocket and whispering, "Someone will call an eight and you must produce these. At least, you must try, my love." And then, as he stepped back, saying a touch more loudly for the benefit of the two gentlemen who'd flicked their glances in his direction, "Excuse me, madam, I trust I didn't step on your foot," before he'd disappeared into the crowd.

"Miss Cathie!"

Still caught up in the horror of what Hugo had unwittingly done, Charity turned at the familiar tone. Rough yet cultured, demanding yet steeped in cloying civility, she looked up to see Mr Cyril Adams beckoning to her from across the room.

"Where's my Lady Luck, eh? Ah, there she is! Come this way, please. To the table, yes!"

A pathway was immediately made for her. Charity turned back in panic to Rosetta and Emily who halted their conversation with their admiring male contingent and nodded encouragingly at her before Rosetta slipped into her wake. "Don't worry, Charity. I'm here. The dice are in your pocket. You — or someone else — will find a way to use them."

Charity opened her mouth to explain the disaster but her friend gave her a gentle push towards Cyril, saying, "You'll play it just right. Don't you worry."

Don't worry? How could she not when they were all doomed? What had Hugo done?

Rosetta and Emily blithely imagined everything was set up for success. Hugo had such hopes, too, as she took her place, once again beside the most hated man in the room.

But everything was ruined and Charity was a jelly of fear. Now what would happen? How could she possibly save Hugo from the terrible fate that awaited him in India? He was about to sink himself even further.

Mr Adams tipped her chin and pinched her cheek as if she were a plaything, smiling at her in such a fashion that suggested she should be grateful for his attention.

She swallowed and tried to respond as she knew she ought. How could one as inexperienced as she summon up bravado she didn't have for the 'right' kind of smile? The new girls at Madame Chambon's were all instructed in the 'right' way to do all manner of things for the gentleman but because of Charity's special status, she'd been spared from anything more than verbal information.

"Please don't ask me to throw, sir," she pleaded. "It's not beginner's luck anymore. I'll throw badly...not what you want...and then you'll be cross."

"Cross?" His voice sounded too loud. Too indulgent, as if he were decades older and she just a child. Indeed, he stroked her cheek as if she were one and as his hand lingered to stroke the corner of her mouth, Charity caught a flash of hurt and anger as Hugo stepped into view.

Please don't say anything that will implicate we're together, Charity begged him with her eyes before she turned a weak smile upon Cyril. Surely Hugo would not be so stupid?

"How could I be cross with an angel?" Mr Adams asked to the sound of corroborating murmurs. It was as if the gentlemen surrounding them were united in their paternalism. "Now! I want another nine!"

Charity glanced at the faces ranged about her. There was the northerner, glowering, down on his luck, apparently, hoping for the dice to turn against his cocky opponent. Beside him, the third player — the pale sandy-haired gentleman who'd drawn her into his orbit earlier — looked warily at Charity. Communicating with her?

She looked down at the table, at her shaking free hand, then up again at the speculation on the faces of the other gentlemen. Everyone here knew Cyril was a cheat. It was whispered by more than just those who had fallen foul of him.

Rosetta had indicated that someone was about to call him out on it.

Please, let it not be Hugo.

Now she was required to throw the dice that Cyril had pressed into her hand.

A nine!

Cyril crowed his triumph amidst soft murmurings as the two cubes rolled gently across the table top.

Of course, she'd thrown a nine. He'd supplied the dice.

Cyril had one more throw. Charity could barely attend to what was happening yet she must. Her mind was a muddle. Just as the dice in her pocket were. Unwittingly, Hugo had mixed the dice — though how could she remove them from her pocket in front of such a crowd? It never would have worked.

"I call on Lady Luck to throw me another nine."

Cyril stood with his chest puffed out, no doubt in anticipation that the game was his. Beside him, the sandy-haired gentleman exchanged a quick look with Rosetta and opened his mouth to speak.

To demand a change of dice, Charity assumed. The dice that Rosetta had slipped into Charity's pocket.

A voice from the crowd cut in. "I challenge you to throw with dice not supplied by you, Mr Adams!"

Hugo!

There was a shocked silence. A few more gentlemen joined those at the table, flanking the northerner and the pale gentleman who was playing Cyril and who, Charity saw, sent a distinctly panicked look at Rosetta now standing at Charity's left shoulder.

"Are you calling me a cheat?"

Charity gasped and raised her head to see Cyril's eyes narrowed with anger.

"My own cousin? Who owes me such a grand sum?" His nostrils flared. "Why, of course, you'd say it, wouldn't you?" He made a noise of disgust, turning to the rest of the company as if expecting them to refute such a claim.

No one did.

"Have the girl pick her own dice," came a voice from somewhere and she twisted her head and saw it was the sandy-haired gentleman. He sent her an encouraging nod. He'd no doubt assumed the dice Rosetta had supplied were still in her pocket.

But then someone from the crowd was

handing her two cubes and voices were calling across the table, "Throw it, young lady! Throw it! See if he gets his nine."

What choice did she have?

So, she tossed and the dice rolled over the green baize table top with agonising slowness. A five…

Luck would not favour a four. It couldn't. Only the Devil's own luck.

But with a cry of triumph that's what it appeared Cyril had for a collective gasp rang out as the second die raised a triumphant four to the sky.

For a split-second, Cyril seemed as disbelieving as the rest of them, before he crowed with laughter. "By God, if you won't rue the day you slandered me, Hugo!" he said before deferring to the northerner adding, "Unless you'd like to cut your losses or, default to mine own beloved cousin. Come Hugo, I dare you to reverse my colleague's losing streak. Take on his losses and turn them around to victory, I dare you. Everything on this throw, eh?"

Charity was so focussed on the exchange that she hardly realised the fact that Rosetta was insinuating into her palm the dice she'd retrieved from Charity's pocket. The dice she'd put there ready for the moment when her partner in crime, called his number. Who knew what number he'd call but Rosetta believed the dice she'd retrieved would answer.

But unbelievably Hugo was stepping forward. It was the moment he'd engineered. The moment he'd intended Charity to work with him.

"Accepted," said Hugo with a surprising degree of confidence after the briefest conferring with the man whom Cyril was beating soundly. "I call eight."

Charity tried to shake her head. Tried to warn him with her eyes. She had no idea what the dice would roll. But Hugo must have seen her thrust her hand into her skirt pocket; he must have thought confidently that she had the means to restore his fortunes. Their fortunes.

But the dice Emily had put there had been joined by Hugo's. She had no way of knowing which were which and now Hugo was confidently calling an eight. An eight to counteract his cheating cousin because he'd been pushed to the brink and cheating — yes, cheating! — was the only way he thought he could redress matters.

She could barely bring herself to watch. Hugo was about to compound the worst mistake of his life and Charity could only stand by and stare, helplessly.

"And now my lady luck will roll for you, cousin." With a shrug, Cyril draped his arm about Charity just as a pair of dice were pushed into her hands. The dice from her pocket? From the table?

It seemed Hugo hadn't moved but his gaze was fixed on the cubes in Charity's palm. Now she was about a play and if she threw anything other than an eight, she'd effectively wipe away another fortune that rightfully belonged to Hugo. No, not a fortune. He'd be plunging him into debt from which it would take years to extricate himself.

"Five and four certainly does not make eight!" Cyril crowed. "I declare myself the winner. Hugo, are you ready to settle up?"

He dropped a careless kiss upon Charity's cheek. It was like an oily rag to a flame.

With a cry of rage, Hugo threw himself across the table scattering people, coins, and banknotes in his wake before he was restrained by a couple of burly fellows who'd appeared seemingly from the woodwork.

CHAPTER 7

$\mathcal{C}$yril had summoned them. Charity had seen the muted command from the corner of her eye though her horrified focus had been on Hugo. He'd wanted to salvage their terrible situation. He'd wanted mostly to do it for Charity. And yet together they had made everything so much worse.

Now what could Charity do? She was frozen to the spot, Cyril's hand caressing the inside of her arm while Hugo was being dragged backwards like an animal, his protests that Cyril had cheated drowned out by Cyril's triumphant response that he'd had no part in the rolling of the dice and why didn't he take it up with Lady Luck.

And just as Hugo was borne out of the double doors, Charity was swung round in Cyril's arms, his delight at his success over his cousin prompting him to kiss her soundly on the mouth before he pushed a drink into her hand and bade her celebrate his success.

She choked on the fizzing liquid, her eyes watering, and her nose twitching which evinced a roar of delight from Cyril.

"Why, aren't you too darling for words? You really *are* a novice."

He didn't remove his hateful grasp as he seemed to regard her with new interest. Then, taking her hand, he led her towards the doorway.

"What are you doing?" Charity squeaked.

"I'm going to reward you," he said loudly, grinning at the gentlemen about him. "You've done well for me and I don't want to let you go just yet."

"I haven't rewarded you. It was luck. Pure chance!" Charity cried. "I...I don't want to leave my friends and go with you."

"Of course, you do," he said, his tone genial

as if her protests meant nothing. Which of course they didn't. "Here. Give them a wave. They're Madame Chambon's girls, aren't they? I recognise one of them. Yes, wave to them and they can proudly report back to Madame that you're in safe hands. In the hands of a very rich man who is very satisfied with what you have done for him tonight." Cyril jerked his head in recognition of Rosetta and Emily who were smiling at him as if they were only too pleased for Charity.

What could she do? She stumbled down the stairs and out into the fresh air, the wind cooling her tear-stained cheeks as she tried to gather her wits. Where was Hugo? Was he all right?

Now, she was on Cyril's arm, confused, helpless. Rosetta and Emily claimed she should go with him to discover what she could, but it was fanciful to think anything good could come of it.

Charity knew she should break free and run. Why had she not when Cyril had assisted her into her cloak in the lobby? The white street, through the doors, had beckoned and for one moment she'd entertained the thought.

But then the carriage had drawn up at the bottom of the stairs.

And there was Cyril, running lightly down the steps to open the door; waiting for her just as the strange gentleman had stood waiting for her mother more than twelve years ago.

Waiting with a smile in his eyes and the promise of a different future.

Until Charity's mother had tugged at Charity's hand, turning on a sob, forcing Charity back up the stairs and into the grand country house where she worked and where she'd taken her daughter, secretly, for the day.

Leaving the gentleman whom Charity had seen kiss her mother in the shadows, just minutes before.

She remembered how strongly she'd wanted that 'different future' the gentleman had promised them after he'd pressed a coin into her palm.

And she remembered, too, how he'd shouted after them: "It's your choice! If you

don't come with me now, I will never acknowledge that I have a daughter!"

Well, Charity wanted a different future,
now, though she wasn't sure this one would
answer.

With sudden resolve she gripped Cyril's
arm and stepped towards the vehicle.
"Where are we going?" she asked him, her
breath frosting in the cold air, glad that her
voice sounded stronger than she thought it
might. Maybe she *could* do this. Maybe she
could be of some help to Hugo.

She rubbed her hands together to keep
them warm.

Of course it was nonsense to think she
could find a book of blackmail but perhaps
she could find some way to appeal to Cyril
if they were in private. Right now, it seemed
her only chance.

"Somewhere we can be comfortable."

"To your townhouse?"

He looked down at her as he helped her
into the vehicle. "You are a fetching little
thing, aren't you? What did you say your
name was?"

Charity hesitated a moment as she tried

to remember the moniker agreed upon by Rosetta and Emily.

"Cathie."

"Well, Cathie, we could go to a nice rooming house, I rather thought."

She nodded. "Probably best," she agreed. "There are great risks in taking a girl like me to your townhouse. What would the servants say?" She forced herself to look impish.

"It's of no consequence what my servants think," he said with a touch of vinegar. "I'm master of my domain."

Charity said nothing more, afraid that it might fuel a desire on Cyril's part to prove himself master of *her* — which he no doubt was going to *try* to do, anyway.

When they stopped in front of a row of elegant townhouses, she raised her eyebrows as she craned her head to look at her surroundings. "What a lovely place," she asked. "Who does it belong to?"

"It's mine," said Cyril. "And I'm taking you through the front door, Cathie, my love." He rapped loudly. "Brown, my butler, will admit us. See if he betrays his true feelings when he takes our coats. If he does, I'll get a new one."

"A new coat?" Charity asked without thinking and he roared with laughter. "A new butler. Ah, Brown, I'm sure the fire has been built up in my room so it's cosy and welcoming." He turned to Charity as he led her along the corridor. "In here. Good, I see the staff are frightened enough to stay up until the small hours. Now, make yourself comfortable."

Charity stared at the large four-poster bed at which he was pointing.

"Come on, now. Hop up. You know I can afford you — or rather, I can afford Madame's exorbitant charges thanks to your help this evening." He chuckled as he brandished a wad of notes from an inner pocket.

"On the...bed?" Her voice shook and she took a step back towards the door. She couldn't do this, after all. No, she wouldn't. What had she been thinking?

An image of Hugo's stricken face swept away her fears for her own wellbeing. How could she do this to him?

How could she *not* do this *for* him?

Yet, how ill-equipped was she to carry out any useful investigative work when she had no idea what she was looking for. How could she appeal to Cyril's better nature when he had none?

She was not about to sacrifice herself for any of Rosetta or Emily's friends. What might Cyril do if he caught her snooping? Even if she asked some pertinent questions it would only take one wrong step to arouse his suspicions and matters would be even worse for Hugo — not to mention herself.

"My dear girl, are you really so naïve? Is this truly your first time?"

Charity pressed her lips together and gave the slightest of nods. Would he be kinder if that's what he thought? But, perhaps for once in her life, she could be other than passive. The time had come, she decided, when she really must seize the next opportunity, after all, and run for her life. Her virtue.

He held out his hand as if he were coaxing a small animal closer.

Charity certainly felt as vulnerable as a

small animal. In the sights of this hunter, she had nowhere to run.

Only, she *could* run. There was an opportunity. The door was not locked and she could reach it faster than Cyril could.

"Come, Cathie, I'll be gentle. I promise."

Charity drew in a shuddering breath as she clutched her hand to her chest.

"Come, my dear. Don't be afraid." His smug, smiling face came closer.

He touched her lips with his forefinger and it took every effort for Charity not to bite it off.

Instead, she reared back, spun on her heel and took off into the corridor, stopping a fateful second to take stock of her bearings.

Of course, he was too quick for her and when he pushed her back into the room and closed the door behind them, then locked it, Charity expected the worst. He had unfettered access to her now. And he was cruel. He'd make her pay. She'd heard of his type. Heard about *him*.

She'd been a fool to run. Now he'd push her against the wall and kiss her like she'd watched her mother being kissed. Could she pretend to enjoy it, as her mother had pretended? At first, Charity had thought she *was* willing until her mother had broken apart at Charity's shout, weeping that the gentleman ruined her life.

Though, nevertheless, her mother had still nearly gone with him.

How confusing it had been. How confusing those memories still were.

"Good lord, I believe those tears are real."

She didn't expect it when Cyril dropped his hands from her shoulders, the snarl softening, his tawny eyes registering confusion rather than flashing danger. No, she'd expected to be given no quarter and was sure this was just an act.

"Of course they're real. I'm not that good an actress," she mumbled, crossing her hands over her chest and drawing herself up, rigidly. She sank against the curtains at the window. She was his prisoner now. He believed he was entitled to her and she had no recourse. "Do what you must to me," she said, woodenly. "I won't scream and rouse the servants."

He looked surprised as he stood in front of her, his expression one of curiosity. "Well, I've never bedded a virgin before and I can't decide whether to make you scream out of respect for my prowess or because you can't bear for me to leave you once I'm done."

"Just do it and get it over and done with," Charity ground out, finishing on a sob. What would her beloved think if he could see her now? Would she tell him? No, his pride would be too damaged. He couldn't help her so why torment him more than he was already?

He took her hand and led her to the sofa in front of the fire. "A glass of champagne does wonders to bolster the spirits though I personally prefer brandy," he said, pulling on the bell-rope and issuing orders to Brown to fetch a bottle from the cellars. "Now, tell me why you're so afraid."

"Because...you're putting on an act." Charity didn't mind telling it to his face as she held her hand against her chest. "As soon as you think you've calmed me so I won't scream, you'll have your way with me."

"And you don't want that? *Really?*" He pressed a flute of champagne into her hand as he led her closer to the fire, helping her into a comfortable chair. He seemed calmer now. Less flushed and, she hoped, less drunk. Or would she fare better if he was more drunk? There was always the chance he might pass out, then.

Nervously she plucked at her skirts. "Of course I don't. I don't know you."

"I might point out that this is your job. Your chosen way to earn a living. However, we're getting to know each other now. So, Cathie, what brought you to the Red Door tonight?"

She opened her mouth in shock. Would it be folly to mention Hugo?

"My friends from Madame Chambon's brought me."

"They're teaching you the tricks of the trade, are they? Nice girls?"

Charity nodded as he moved behind her. "They'll be worried about me."

"But you're in safe hands. They know where you are." To emphasise his point, he gently contoured her shoulders then stroked her neck. Charity closed her eyes as he reached her face. Submit. Submit. That's what she had to do.

"How nice to have someone who cares even a fig for you." He sighed. "I don't."

"Well, I don't expect you to. That's why I'm — "

"I'm not talking about you." He moved around to stand in front of her so he could see her. "No one cares a fig about *me*. Never did."

Charity knew this wasn't true. His grandfather had left him a fortune. He'd be receiving it in a few months.

"Is that why you must gamble? Because you'll be destitute unless you win every time? Regardless of the cost?" She looked around her pointedly. "You really have no one else to look to?"

"I had a father and a mother, like everyone else, naturally." He chuckled as he took a seat in the wing back chair opposite. "Can't remember my mother as she died when I was born. My father? Well, the less said about him, the better. A cold, ruthless man. They say blood will out. What hope do I have? Thank goodness he's about to head off to the family estates in India with my cousin. I thought I'd have to face that dastardly duty but thank God I got lucky at the cards and passed the baton to Hugo."

And thank God Cyril didn't know what Hugo was to Charity, since he clearly had so little love for his cousin. No, she decided, appealing to his better nature would not work. Instead, she said, "My father was a gambler and I've never felt the pull."

He looked surprised. "He was, was he? And what was your father, if you don't mind my asking?" He was toying with her now. "Let me guess. You speak decently enough. I'd say he was…a tutor? Yes, I do like guessing games. Tell me I'm right."

"No, but my mother was a governess."

"A governess, eh? A penniless, beautiful governess. I wonder who your father was, then? I was in love with my governess when I was sixteen. I'd have married her if I'd been able to. Were they star-crossed lovers, like we were?"

"He was a gentleman."

"A gambler and a gentleman who'd be rolling in his grave if he saw you now."

"He's not dead."

Cyril looked surprised. "So, your father is a gentleman and yet you earn your living by lying with the likes of me."

Charity shrugged. His words hurt but she said, "What else can a girl do when she has no other means of earning her keep? Besides, my father refused to acknowledge me. At least, he refused to do so when I was eight."

"So, you know who he is?"

Charity nodded. Good lord, had she really told him all this? She'd simply been too outraged by his pathetic claim that no one loved him. As if he were the only one.

"Who is he?"

"I'm not telling you that."

"That's because it's all one big tall tale to make you seem more impressive than you really are. You're from the gutter." He looked disappointed. "Girls like you don't tell the truth."

"Because we *deserve* to be in the gutter? And that's how you'd treat us?" Charity felt the rage tingling in her extremities. "I think it makes men feel strong to beat down those more vulnerable. Mostly, it's the men who've been treated badly in their own lives. That's what the girls tell me at Madame Chambon's."

"Oh, really?" He tapped his fingers on the arm of the sofa as if deciding what to say or do. "Well, your job is to please me," he said finally. He indicated her glass. "Drink up, Cathie. I'm not feeling as kindly towards you as I was."

His eyes were dark and brooding. Charity shivered. What had made her speak so unwisely to such a dangerous bully as Cyril.

"So you've changed your mind again? Instead of being considerate and making this a first time to remember — and make me regard you kindly and favour you above all my other clients, you think violence is preferable? That it will give you the upper hand, which of course it will?" Charity pushed out her chest. "That is the coward's way. That's what the girls all tell me. It's the cowards and the bullies who use force and strength whereas it's the men who use kindness who are given the best treatment at Madame's, I can assure you."

"Good God, will you stop talking!" Unexpectedly, Cyril rose to his feet, sweeping his glass from the table with an angry thrust of his arm. "There is no goodness in me so why should I waste my time trying to be kind?"

Charity shrank against the arm of the sofa as he paced in front of the fire. Her heart was pounding now. He was volatile. Unpredictable. She didn't have the measure of him. "Has no one ever been kind to you?" she ventured. She'd touched a nerve and perhaps it was unwise to pursue this line, but she thought she understood him a little better now.

"Not my father."

"Nor mine to me."

"I never knew my mother."

"Mine sent me to look after an imbecile

aunt. That was fun, too." Charity said with heavy irony.

There was a slight pause, then Cyril suddenly let out an unexpected laugh as he rose from throwing a log on the fire. "Did you really conjure that up to best my tale of woe?"

"No, it's true. I've spent most of my life in thankless drudgery before I found myself at Madame Chambon's, after I was tricked there, thinking I was applying for work as a servant. Yet, for the first time in my life, I made friends. Women who had suffered cruelty, as I had, and who were kind to me."

Cyril looked at her strangely. He'd stopped what he was doing and was now breathing heavily, his mouth working as if a torrent of words would tumble out at any moment, yet he was holding it all in. Finally, he strode toward the table and snatched up his brandy.

"Do you really need that?" Charity asked. "You're bosky, as it is. I suppose you're fortifying yourself for…"

"I do not need you to tell me what to do." His words held an edge of dangerous quiet.

Charity steeled herself against the inevitable. He'd hurt her, regardless of what she said. The other girls had plenty of stories about men who liked to tell a girl with the back of their hands when they were displeased.

She faced him squarely, drawing back her shoulders. Preparing herself. Managing to keep the terrible fear inside her at bay. It was naïve foolishness and false bravado which had led her into this danger. She had no one but herself to blame.

Dear Lord, why had she not planned this better?

She closed her eyes and gripped the sofa's arm rest. Yes, it was better that she closed her eyes and make her body pliant and accessible so that she'd suffer the least amount of pain. That's what the girls at Madame's had told her she should do. They'd said she must transport her mind to another realm. Some of the girls swore it was this which enabled them to earn the only living available to them.

Silence. It was a terrifying prelude.

She could hear only the clock ticking.

Her surroundings were a black void with just her thoughts whirling around her head.

She shifted a little. Still waiting.

If she could concentrate on the good things she'd once looked forward to with Hugo, perhaps she wouldn't even notice his assault on her body; though in her heart she knew it would be the beginning of the corrosive destruction of her very being, the very essence of her.

Charity, the innocent, was not going to get her fairytale with the happy ending, after all, but she must survive. And she had only herself to blame. Her foolishness had brought her right into this trap. The girl that Madame had cossetted, had been the embodiment of the dream they'd all had: that a client would fall in love with them; a client worthy of their affections, and that a partnership built on mutual love and trust and exclusivity would end their sordid lives selling the only commodity they had.

She became conscious, now, of the sound of her breathing, loud in her ears. Her hands were clammy and her world was black as she kept trying to imagine herself into another one, only to slip back into the terrible present.

But the time stretched out and still, he didn't make his move as she'd expected.

Confused, she opened her eyes and found him staring at her. As if he, too, was unsure what to do.

He was standing near her, towering above her, his hard eyes trained on her.

After she opened her eyes, he put out his hand and touched her shoulder.

"Nice," he whispered, stroking her bare skin. A light crept into his eyes and his lips turned up. "You're shivering. You like it then?"

Charity focused every bit of loathing into her response. "I hate it.

He looked surprised before his eyes darted to the sideboard. "I'm paying you handsomely," he said, indicating what was, indeed, a sum tucked beneath the brandy bottle that would keep her for a week.

"I don't want your money," she whispered. "I want my freedom."

He continued to stroke her, though

more tentatively now as he asked, clearly offended, "You dislike me that much?"

"I despise you."

Now, he stopped the rhythmic movement of his hand that had been tracing the line of her décolletage and regarded her with a look that suggested he didn't know whether to be outraged rather than merely offended.

Either way, he'd resort to violence. This is what men did when they were insulted. Charity watched the play of emotions cross his narrow, angry face. She began the count-down in her head.

And then the odd, tense silence was broken by the sound of running footsteps in the corridor, followed by a cry of outrage as Hugo burst through the doors, knocking aside a table as he hurled himself upon Cyril.

Charity was quick-witted enough to dart behind a large armchair by the fire as the two men crashed to the floor.

"Fiend!" cried her beloved, gentle Hugo as he thrust his knee in the small of Cyril's back and wrenched his arm behind him. His chest rose and fell and his eyes were wild as Charity had never seen them. "I'll kill you if you've laid a hand on her!"

"She came willingly enough!" Cyril snarled, letting out a cry of pain as Hugo slammed his head upon the floor.

"Hugo, stop!" cried Charity as the blood from Cyril's nose sprayed over the rug.

Cyril's voice was muffled but she still felt the sting of his retort. "Good God! So *she's* your little fancy piece. I had no idea." He let out a surprised laugh, truncated with a cry of pain as Hugo slammed his head down upon the floor once more.

CHAPTER 8

*H*ugo took her to their special place. A house where no questions were ever asked. A house run by a kind matron who, perhaps, had her own reasons for turning a blind eye but who kept a neat, unremarkable lodging house where the rooms were clean and the bed was comfortable.

"I didn't want to go with him," Charity wept after Hugo had shut out the world and now cradled her against his chest in their warm, comfortable bed.

"My poor darling, I know that." Hugo's voice was thick with what Charity understood now were tears as she raised her head to look at him. They clung to his lashes but his voice was steady though his breathing was laboured. "Did he hurt you? Dear God, I'll kill him! I'll — "

Charity shook her head as she raised her finger to his lips. "No, my love, he didn't touch me. Well, only my shoulder. I promise you! You came just in time."

She felt some of the tension drain out of him though his words were full of self-recrimination. "How will I protect you when I'm gone, Charity?" It was almost a cry of despair. "What will become of you? I can't guarantee your security for the many months I'll be away."

"But you can guarantee my happiness now," Charity whispered, tugging at the button that secured his collar. She'd soothe the worry from him as only she knew how. In the morning he'd be gone and Charity would be at the mercy of the world.

But for a few hours tonight, she could try and forget that. They both could.

And she'd do her very best to bolster his hopes that she would be safe.

He cupped her cheek and kissed her tenderly while Charity stroked his strong, young chest before wrapping her arms tightly about him.

"I will never forget you, Hugo," she promised, revelling in the warmth and weight of him. He might be gentle but he was well built and well endowed. She might be innocent of other men but she knew her Hugo was more the lover than any of the gentlemen callers her friends entertained.

And more passionate.

"I won't let you," he vowed, his voice tight with promise. "You think I won't come back to you? That I'll fail in my promise to ensure your upkeep?" He rose above her on one elbow, his eyes bright. "I have managed, at least, to provide for you for the first two months I'm away. Madame has the money in trust so that you'll not be turned into the street. I anticipate that by that time I'll have managed to send you my wages after my first couple of months away. And I'll write every day, Charity." He took a deep breath. "I swear to you that in two years I will come back to marry you."

"A Christmas wedding," sighed Charity

though she didn't believe it. Still, it's what he needed to believe when she farewelled him. He could face whatever hardships were in store if he truly thought he'd ensured Charity's protection and that, not only would he be still alive and wanting to marry her in two years, he'd be allowed to.

Family pressure was a very powerful force. Old Mr Adams was not going to let his son marry a girl from the gutter without a fight, even if Hugo was a man of independent means.

"Yes, a Christmas wedding," Hugo promised, as he rose over her, smiling that sweet gentle smile that never failed to make her insides roil with love and excitement as he stroked her into arousal. For the moment, he was hers. She felt he always would be, even if he never came back.

"With mistletoe in my bouquet," she whispered, gilding the dream they both needed to pretend, for now, would become a reality.

"And my mother's locket around your neck." His fingers brushed across her throat and she shivered with anticipation as he positioned himself at her entrance. "For you *will* be accepted as my worthy wife, my precious girl. My father will — "

She stayed his words with her forefinger, gently trailing it across his cheek as she shook her head. "Your father will never accept me, Hugo, but I don't need that."

"But *I* do."

Charity drew in a breath and closed her eyes as he entered her.

With a sigh of ecstasy he whispered, "I swear on my life that I will come back and marry you, my darling."

CHAPTER 9

"Just your trunks to seal, sir, and you're ready to sail." Keating, the butler stood to attention, waiting for the order as Hugo entered the drawing room. He would not be taking much. Two sturdy trunks were all he needed.

"This will be the making of you, my boy," his father said, rising from his chair by the fire and walking towards him. He'd come down from the country, ostensibly to farewell his only child though Hugo thought it more likely that it was to ensure that Hugo would be travelling alone. His father didn't even trust his brother to ensure Hugo brought aboard no stowaways.

Hugo nodded briefly but made no reply as he went to the writing desk where he'd been working on his last drawings and poems for Charity.

"What have you got there?" His father's tone was genial as he moved to stand behind him.

Hugo ignored him. If his father wanted tacit forgiveness from his son he'd not get it. Hugo would never forgive him for his collusion with Cyril. The beatings and other punishments were forgivable. But not this. His father had garnished a deal that would make Hugo beholden to him; make him his slave. And Cyril had been only too happy to oblige. Hugo had always despised his cousin but he despised his father more.

"A fine drawing. Very fine." His father nodded at the finely rendered head and shoulders drawing of Charity. "She's a beauty, to be sure, and you've captured that."

Hugo studied his last work of art. The last picture that perhaps he'd ever draw of

Charity when it was just the two of them together. The wistfulness of her expression had tugged at his heartstrings when he'd caught her gazing out of the window while Hugo had been telling her about his visit to Madame's. A visit during which he'd gone through every possibility to ensure Charity was employed as anything other than a slave to the gentlemen who stepped over the threshold.

When he'd tried to reassure Charity she'd simply smiled. He knew she didn't believe him but he had to try and keep up the pretence, if only to keep up her hopes when hope was all she had.

A woman had few options if she didn't have connections. A woman without financial independence was at the mercy of the world.

And if her name were tarnished, or if she had lost her reputation; if she had no references to recommend her to an employer. Then all she had to barter was her body.

Charity was like so many women, Hugo thought bitterly, though God knew it was hardly her fault.

"A beauty, I'm the first to admit. And no doubt obliging and good-natured. Everything a man could desire in a mistress."

Hugo remained tight-lipped, moving away as his father put out his hand to see the drawing better. The stack of drawings slipped from his hands and floated to the floor. More than a dozen sketches and paintings of Charity spread about them, her beauty painful to behold right now.

There was the only girl he'd ever loved gazing at the painter with gentle trust in one. Or with heart-breaking hauteur in another. Her hair was tumbled and her bosom a touch too much in evidence in another but the one he reached for first depicted her in a ballgown, every inch the equal of the heiress his father would have him marry. Yes, she had grace and dignity to equal any one of them.

"You'll thank me one day, boy."

Hugo turned at the low growl, making no attempt to mask his dislike.

"If anything happens to her when I'm gone I'll despise you 'til the day I die," he said under his breath, before bending to gather up the rest of the drawings.

His father stopped him when Hugo would have brushed past him and out of the door for there was one final task he had to do before he sailed.

"I can see the attraction, Hugo, for you paint true to life. But she'd drag you down. And you'd come to resent her for it. What basis is that for a marriage? When you'd be bound to her for life?"

Hugo considered him a moment. His father had had the benefit of an education but he'd never been considered on an equal footing with his schoolfellows. He wanted this for his son more than he wanted anything else; hence the tortuous years at Eton, the miserable rounds of trying to mould him into the man his father wanted him to become.

"I should not care where she dragged me so long as she was my wife."

The chasm between them had never yawned so deep. In the middle of a room boasting the trappings of wealth without softness, expense without taste, his father

was as much a victim of his success as gen-
erations before him had been of their
poverty.

He ran a hand through his thick white
hair and his lustrous, salt and pepper moustache twitched. His watery blue eyes regarded Hugo with dislike. "I hope she
knows you'll not get a penny of your grandfather's fortune if you wed her in haste before you leave."

"Oh, she knows it well. But in less than
two years I'll be free to do as I choose."
Hugo turned at the door. "And I'll be right
back here. In London. Begging her to make
me the happiest man alive and marry me.
Romantic tosh, eh, father?" Hugo offered
him a parting smile. Or, at least, the parody
of one. "I'm the first to admit that it is in-
convenient to have a heart, at times." He
pushed back his shoulders. "At least I can
live with *my* conscience. Now, if you'll excuse me."

He decided against taking a hackney the
few blocks to his cousin's townhouse and
when he arrived Cyril was in the hallway
donning his hat and coat.

"A good thing I caught you," Hugo said, amused at the flare of anger in the other man's face and the way Cyril's hand went protectively to his nose, still swollen after the previous night.

"I hadn't expected to see you again." Cyril turned his back to pick up his umbrella before heading down the steps to the street.

"You weren't going to see me off?" Hugo pretended surprise. "Good riddance and all that? Leaving you to enjoy what I can't take with me?" He lengthened his stride so he was level with his cousin before gripping his elbow and jerking him so he was facing him, pressing him against a brick wall beneath an old bridge. Passersby looked at them strangely.

"I swear that if you touch Charity...if you cause her a single moment's anxiety, then yesterday will be nothing compared with the way I'll make sure you suffer when I return home."

"You know I didn't touch her yesterday, either." Cyril sounded sulky as he pulled back his arm and carried on walking.

"Not for want of trying. I heard you visited Madame Chambon's the very day after I told Charity I had to leave."

"Curiosity. What well-intentioned cousin wouldn't want to see if such a girl could be as pure and true as she was made out to be?"

"She's known only me." Hugo wasn't saying it to boast. He couldn't bear the idea that anyone should imagine that what he and Charity shared was any less pure than a union sanctified by God. "And one day she will be my wife." He looked at his cousin while he fought the poison within him. "Just remember that. Thanks to you, that day will be longer coming than I intended." He drew in a breath through his nose, his expression, he hoped, reflecting the force of his hatred. "Regardless of my father's desires to the contrary, and your collusion, it will happen."

Cyril seemed disinclined to be engaged. Taking advantage of a cooper's wagon lumbering by, he dashed in front of it, swinging around angrily when Hugo followed him. They'd reached a small, fenced park into which Hugo was channelling him so as to be out of the public eye.

"For God's sake, Hugo, leave it and go! As always, I get the blame!"

Hugo clenched his fists while he fought his temper. He'd never been quick to anger, unlike Cyril, but tomorrow he'd be sailing to a land far from Charity and the world he wanted to inhabit with her. His dreams had been cruelly dashed and his nemesis was before him.

He glared at Cyril. "It might have been Papa who put you up to this but you were a willing party. I don't know what, exactly, he asked you to do but you leapt at the first opportunity to ruin me. Why? So, my father would have an excuse to send me away?" He heard his voice shake and was angry at himself. Why should he care that Cyril, with his broad shoulders, glib tongue, and clever cunning was far more the kind of son his father wanted than the dreamy, namby-pamby boy he'd derided from the cradle.

Hugo couldn't help himself. He'd tried to have as little as possible to do with Cyril and the society he kept. He'd tried to hold himself to higher ideals. Ideals which should have precluded him saying bitterly, "Well, hasn't he always favoured you? And weren't you so willing to get into his good books by destroying what I had with Charity? Papa couldn't bear that I should marry a girl he considered as lowly as his own mother but you were the first to step up and do his bidding. You didn't care that you were hurting a girl who was tricked into crossing Madame Chambon's threshold. A girl whose father came from the very world into which our own fathers wish to be accepted. Ironic, isn't it? In terms of the blood that runs through her veins, Charity is better born than either of us. Yet, because she's a woman and she's illegitimate, she has none of the protections or ability to forge her own way in life, that we take for granted."

"God, but you're insufferably self-righteous, Hugo!" Cyril flung at him as he turned to confront his cousin. "I couldn't care less about any of this! Not who you marry or where she comes from or what your father wants or doesn't want for you." He threw out his arms in frustration, his umbrella spinning in the air. "The only reason I agreed to help your father see you sink a fortune was so that *I* wouldn't be forced to spend the next year in a God-forsaken country learning the family trade. It'd be bad enough having to leave the comforts of London but having to spend any time in close proximity with my father would be like living a thousand deaths."

Hugo squared his shoulders. "And you think *I* deserve that?"

"At least he won't beat you senseless at every opportunity. I imagine you'll be spared that since you're only a nephew and will be required to get up and do a day's work rather than be made an example of. He has no great expectations of *you*."

He said it as if Hugo had never been considered up to much by the rest of the family. Cyril, by contrast, had enjoyed his rugby, cricket, and boxing.

Hugo chewed his lip. His anger had dissipated somewhat but his uncertainty was as great as ever. "You promise you won't prey on Charity?"

"*Prey* on her? What do you think I am? A monster as bad as my father?" He gave a short laugh. "I might be a cheat and a bounder but I don't go about forcing myself on vulnerable females and defiling any pretty thing that takes my fancy." He hesitated. "I'm the first to admit that she's a fine filly, your Charity. A real stunner. What she sees in you, I can't imagine."

"I can't either," Hugo said, dolefully, turning to leave this unsatisfactory conversation.

But the change in Cyril's tone when he next spoke was far from reassuring.

"However, old fellow, if your sweet Charity chooses to avail herself of the comforts I can provide her which you — *obviously* — will be in no position to, then that's her choice." He chuckled. "How many weeks have you secured for her maintenance? No more than eight, is my guess. Well!" He sighed. "A girl's got to live, hasn't she?"

CHAPTER 10

For just a few moments more, Charity could revel in the warmth of Hugo's body pressed against hers, his overcoat shielding them both as they stood in a sheltered corner of the dockyard.

Then he'd weave his way amongst the throng of tearful well-wishers who crowded the quay and say the no-doubt gruff and loveless farewell that would see him part from his father.

Salty spray borne upon the stiff breeze mingled with the lightly falling snow.

"I will never forget you, Hugo," she whispered into his waistcoat. "Even if I never see you again."

The ground was covered in a blanket of white and the sky was already black, heavy clouds obscuring the stars.

"In two years, I will come back and claim you. One year, if I'm able. You must believe that, Charity."

She believed the sentiment was as heart-felt as it sounded but she didn't believe for one moment that Hugo would appear before her on a cold December day like this one and make good his claim.

"You must do what is best for you, Hugo, and if you meet someone who — "

"No!" He shook his head, his tone fierce. "If I marry, I will marry *you*, Charity. You must believe it. I might have failed miserably to look after you as I should have done but when I come into my inheritance and am master of my finances, I will do whatever it takes to see you shine in a position that does you honour."

He brought his mouth down in a kiss that was as branding as it was tender. Hugo was gentle but he was determined and he was full of fervour.

And so young. Yet what he lacked in age and experience, he made up for in so many other ways.

Reluctantly she stepped back. "You must go, my love. Your father is here. I see him looking for you."

"Then let him see me with you. It might help reinforce the futility of his reasons for sending me away." Hugo took her by the hand and led Charity into the open, just as his father turned in their direction. For a moment they locked glances, then Mr Adams looked away.

With a smile, Hugo brushed her cheek with his hand. "You are exquisite, Charity. I'm never prouder than when I have you by my side." He bent for one final kiss and as Charity wound her arms about his neck she wondered how she'd ever have the strength to let him go.

But she did. And only after he'd started walking away did she let the tears fall.

For Hugo needed to meet his fate with all the fortitude of which he was capable.

~

IT SURELY WAS THE SADDEST CHRISTMAS she'd ever spent. How could she join in the singing with the other girls at Madame Chambon's when the carollers stopped beneath their window? How could she smile at the pink-cheeked children who threw snowballs in the park?

Her heart felt like a cold and empty vessel.

When Maisie tapped on her door and told her that a Mr Adams desired her company, she was torn between bursting out with laughter at his impudence, or weeping at the irony. What would bring this man, of all men, to her threshold after all that had happened?

So, of course, she sent a message making clear how unwelcome he was.

She just hoped and prayed that Madame remained as committed as she had earlier indicated to ensuring Charity's employment did not include crossing any unwelcome thresholds.

Of course, Charity didn't care that her

clothes were the cast-offs of Madame's girls. Or that she'd be engaged in menial drudgery for much of her day. Madame had made it clear that as long as Charity worked hard for her keep, she'd not turn her out. Hugo had paid the brothel-keeper a sum that had made her happy. For now.

However, on the third day, her faith in Madame's uncharacteristic fidelity to Charity's forthcoming Happily Ever After suffered its first major blow.

First of all, a summons to Madame's study was an event to strike fear into any of her girls.

"Mr Adams has paid us his third visit in three days," Madame told her. She'd always been one to come straight to the point and as she stood behind her desk resembling a lamp post through her posture and lack of emotion and the gimlet look in Madame's eyes, Charity felt her faith in Madame's loyalty to her cause, crumble.

"I'm very glad he's not come to see me," Charity said, dropping her eyes to her scuffed boots, swallowing down her fear as the heat rose through her body. Fear. No, terror of why Madame had summoned her.

"Of course he's here to see you, girl! He knows the position you're in and he'll keep coming back. He's a persistent one."

"I have nothing to offer him." Charity raised her chin and sent Madame a warning. Didn't they have an agreement? "Hugo left only *three days ago*."

"And he might never come back. Oh, he's left sufficient for your upkeep for a short while. I'm not about to send you into the jaws of this wolf, or any other, for that matter. But my dear girl, let me just remind you that money doesn't last forever. It doesn't grow on trees. Perhaps it might be as well to cultivate Mr Adams. He is a man of means, after all. And he's made it clear that he intends to be very generous."

Charity couldn't believe what she was hearing. "Cyril was the very reason Hugo has had to leave the country!" she burst out. "I loathe the man. I want nothing to do with him!" She clasped her hands to stop them shaking. "In fact, I *will* have nothing to do with him. Ever!"

For six weeks, Charity heard no more of Mr Cyril Adams. Until one evening, Madame summoned Charity once more and bade her take a seat opposite her impressive wooden desk in her study.

Coins and bills littered the table top and an overflowing pile of receipts spilled out of a silver box.

Yet despite her apparent carelessness with her wealth, Madame knew how much she was worth to the last penny.

"You have one week's rent paid in advance and then you'll need to start paying your way, like the other girls," she said. "That is, unless your sweetheart follows through on his promise to send more my way. I've heard nothing from him. Have you?"

Charity swallowed with difficulty as she shook her head. "I hadn't realised," she whispered.

She slunk back to her room and looked through her wardrobe and her jewellery. When she accepted how little she could recover from her poor selection, she sat on her window seat and stared into the dark street.

In truth, she didn't care about her poverty.

But her heart ached for Hugo and the fact she'd received only one letter from him, two days after he'd left. It was now mid-February and the weather was as cold and gloomy as ever. The days were getting a little longer but each day still felt like a grey prison.

Madame said she had one week left. What did she mean by that? She couldn't force her to work for her as one of her girls. But if Charity refused, then she'd have to find another roof over her head.

Was her interview a veiled threat for the fact that beggars couldn't be choosers? She knew she could make money from Charity.

And, as far as Madame was concerned, money was the only currency that had any meaning.

Charity drew her knees up to her chin and hugged herself closely. She'd held firm to the belief that Hugo would not let her down. Perhaps it had made her complacent.

Now she realised she'd have to make her own plans.

Finding alternative accommodation would have to be her first priority if Madame threw her out into the streets in a week. And it looked like she would, if Charity refused to entertain a paying guest.

But where to start looking? Rosetta had said she'd accompany Charity on her rounds but when the time came, she'd had too late a night to bear her company, so she said.

So, Charity went alone, ill-equipped to drive a bargain with a lodging house keeper. In fact, she was ill-equipped to do anything, she realised. Her whole life had been managed by others.

Halfway through the park on her way to an address that had been recommended to her she was horrified to be accosted by a familiar voice.

Turning, she found Cyril grinning at her as he blocked the entrance gate.

"How very fortuitous. Do you know how

hard I've been trying to get an audience with you?"

"We have nothing to say to each other," Charity said coldly. She wasn't afraid of him out here, in the open.

"A little bird tells me you're fast running out of money and looking for cheaper lodgings."

"And no doubt you have a plan to help me? Except that I don't entertain plans concocted by thieves and swindlers."

Cyril smiled pleasantly. "I'd set you up, you know. Very happily, in fact. You have just the degree of fire I like in a girl. You put up a fight when you're driven but you're essentially a sweet little thing. Meek and mild and pleasing. You're a beauty, too, of course. You'd have to be. I'm a man of discerning tastes."

"And I'm a woman of discerning tastes which is why I wouldn't deal with you if you were the last man alive. I'd sell the clothes off my back before I had to spend a single minute in your company."

He laughed. "I do like the image that conjures up." Then, glancing at the ring on her right hand. "That's worth a pretty penny. Sell that for a month's board and lodging and when your time is up I'll come knocking."

Charity stared at the ring and shook her head. "I can't."

"Not for any price? Surely Hugo would rather you sold the tokens of his regard rather than your body."

Charity jerked her head up. "My father gave it to my mother and I'm not selling it."

Cyril raised his eyebrows. "Ah yes, you did mention he was a man of means and good breeding. Discerning taste, too, it would appear. Forgive me if I remain sceptical. He's a figment of your imagination otherwise you'd petition him, wouldn't you?" He paused. "That is, if you knew who he was."

A spurt of anger quickly turned to indignation. Charity knew she shouldn't engage him. "Of course I do!"

"And does he know who you are?" Cyril sent her a narrowed eyed look that made Charity's ears burn.

She shook her head. "I'm not about to

sink my pride and go to him again. A girl from a brothel? Do you think he'd want anything to do with me, now? He certainly didn't when I was a child." She shrugged. "And while I'd rather not have to sell my ring, I'd do that before I let you touch me. Why, I'd rather sleep with a snake!"

"Harsh. Very harsh. I'm surprised Hugo fell for you with a tongue like that."

Charity sucked in a quick breath. His mention of Hugo was like a whip of pain and disappointment. "Hugo was nothing but kind and gentle with me. I never had cause to speak to him as I do to you."

Hugo nodded. "Yes, most interesting. The way you and my cousin dealt with one another, I mean." He cleared his throat. "The letters that were in the reticule you dropped in my drawing room were a lesson in humility. For me, that is. Tender and loving. I'd never seen sentiments like it between two people. Which is why I thought I could do with a bit of help in my own plans to court a certain young lady. One who would, I'm sure, be far more responsive to the kinds of sweet nothings you and Hugo bandied about with such carelessness." He looked thoughtful. "She certainly didn't exhibit the aversion towards me that conjures up comparisons with disgusting reptiles. I believe I have a chance." Cyril looked pleased with himself. "A few pretty notes would go a long way, I think."

"You can write your own letters." Charity started walking to the gate, even though it meant passing him. Her heart beat harder but he could hardly force her into anything against her wishes, out here in the open. "I'm not doing anything for you," she said over her shoulder, "and I certainly wouldn't want this poor, unsuspecting young lady to think you better than you are. It would be deceitful."

Cyril followed her, arresting her with a hand on her arm.

Charity turned, making no secret of her disgust.

"Think of it as putting me in my place," Cyril laughed. "Wouldn't you love to give me a lesson in humility? Maybe you could make me a better man. After all, how am I supposed to know the kinds of sentiments that come from a good and generous heart when no one has ever shown me?"

Charity shrugged. "I don't think all the teaching in the world can help you with that." She put out her hand. "But I would like my letters back, thank you. They belong to me."

Cyril bowed. "I shall deliver them tonight."

"And I shall have Rosetta accept them on my behalf."

~

SIX DAYS LATER, MADAME AGAIN SUMMONED Charity to her study and Charity went, hoping against hope it meant that Hugo had managed to get a letter sent with even some small means of maintenance that would satisfy Madame for now.

"Emily says you've been looking for alternative accommodation?"

"It went no further than that, Madame. I was hoping…" She tried again. "I thought perhaps Hugo might have sent something."

Madame shook her head. "I've received

nothing. However, that doesn't mean correspondence and succour hasn't been delayed." Her tone gentled. "I don't believe he has forsaken you, Charity. But practicalities must be attended to. Hugo's cousin, Mr Cyril Adams, is here. Now, I am well aware of your feelings towards him but he says he has received news from his father. He thought perhaps you might be interested in seeing him."

"Madame!" Charity stared wildly around the room, then down at her threadbare blue dress.

"You can borrow something finer," said her employer as if that were a matter of concern, but Charity shook her head.

"I'm not entertaining this Mr Adams or...anyone else. I'll leave if I have to. If you want me to. But Madame, I have three days remaining here." Since her last terrifying encounter with Madame she'd made sure to work out how far her rent would last — to the last minute. Madame would know it, too.

"Which is why you'd do well to speak to Mr Adams and find out what his father has to report. His father is with your young man, after all. I thought you'd be only too eager to hear what he has to say.

Of course she did. But not when he'd find other ways to put Charity at a disadvantage. "Tell him to come back when...I have gathered my wits. I have questions, yes, but I'm not yet ready to see him." Charity thought of what she must achieve in the interim so that he would be under no illusions that he could pressure her. She needed a plan that would see her safe and secure. So that regardless of what Cyril offered her or however much he coerced her, she could refuse. Yes, in the morning, she'd find a lodging house or work as a milliner. There must be something she could do that would bring in a little money. Just for as long as it took Hugo to send something. She knew Hugo would be true to his word. It was possible he might not come home to her in two years' time but she did believe three months was too soon for him to have given her up.

Madame came round from the desk and ran her fingers through Charity's hair as she slowly circled her. "You could be one of my most popular girls, Charity. You have the looks and bearing. I've had interest you know. Not just from Mr Adams. Mr Cyril Adams," she amended, her tone thoughtful. Slowly she contoured Charity's bare arms from the wrists up to her decolletage. Charity held her breath. It was just what Madame had done the first night Charity had arrived on her doorstep, late at night, having been sent by, as it transpired, a procuress Charity had met on the coach during the last leg of her long journey from Dorset.

Barely eighteen, Charity had ceased to be useful when her aunt had succumbed to her various maladies and her grandmother had taken in a fourteen-year-old distant relative to look after her in her old age. She'd said it was time for Charity to make her own way in the world.

Little did Charity know what was in store for her when she'd arrived, friendless, in the vast city. She'd thought she'd found a safe haven at Madame's.

Madame was speaking again, Charity realised. But in the brisk tone she usually did. She sounded distant, her thoughts far removed from Charity's concerns, it seemed. "My daughter arrives tonight from France where she has been educated most of her life."

"Oh!"

"You did not know I had a daughter?" Madame smiled. "I haven't seen her in many years. It's true I've missed her but this was no place for her to grow up. Not when I have such plans for her. I've provided well for her and she is a beauty with her rich, auburn hair and her creamy skin." Madame's hands were stroking Charity's neck. "I've become fond of you, Charity, since you've been here. You've touched me with your innocence, reminding me what it must be like to have such faith in the goodness of others. Of that one important person. I'd have liked my Arabella to be soft and innocent like you but she's not. She's proud. She doesn't want to be here, of course. Doesn't want to see her mother, and that pains me." She took a hank of Charity's long, loose hair in each hand and drew it away from her head, assessing Charity as if she were an object.

Then she sighed. "But you're not fiery and proud. You want to stay here, in the only home you've known since you've been in London. I've always prided myself on putting business considerations above all else but I will allow you some latitude, my dear. I, too, like to believe Hugo will return to claim you and his inheritance. I, too, like to believe that his next payment for your upkeep is only days away. If it's not, I'll grant you a week's extension. But that is all. For you have great potential." She smiled at Charity as if she truly were fond of her. "If Hugo comes back, he will want you, regardless of what you have had to do. For though he is a dreamer now, he must understand the practicalities of life. He will understand that a girl has to live."

CHARITY LAY CURLED UP ON HER BED, staring at the ceiling.

"Come in," she said dully, in response to

the knock on the door. She needed what-ever crumbs of friendship Emily or Rosetta could offer her right now.

But instead, Cyril stood upon the threshold.

"What a cosy little nest you've made yourself here," he remarked after a cursory nod in greeting. "My cousin does love his domestic comforts, it appears. The crossing was not kind to him, my father tells me. But then, no one fared well. It was a very rough crossing. May I?" He indicated the chair against the far wall upon which he lowered himself without waiting for a response from Charity.

She, in the meantime, had swung her legs over the side of the bed and was staring at him in outrage.

"Madame said I'd find you here," he said. "Now! Down to business. Hugo tried to send you money but my father suspected as much and is diverting his wages and paying only his necessary in day to day expenses. Sorry." He smiled, clearly not sorry in the least.

"Which means you will need to find a means of survival, won't you?"

Charity's throat went dry. She'd truly not expected this. Not something so utterly dire. She felt the sting of tears at the back of her eyes and tried to speak.

Cyril held up his hand. "I can see that you are overset so just let me speak. I've been thinking of you a great deal, Charity my dear, and I would like to help you."

"Profit by my misery, you mean. Trade on my vulnerability."

He nodded, quite equably, as he pulled a large envelope from his satchel. "Dry your tears, Charity. They won't do you any good, but these should make you happy. At least it proves your Hugo was thinking of you, even if he wasn't able to provide for you."

The joy at seeing nearly two dozen drawings and paintings spill onto the bed made her cry out. And there were letters, too! She picked one up and began to read but Cyril snatched it away. "There'll be time enough for that later. In the meantime, I want to talk to you. Who is your father?"

Charity put her head on one side. "Why is it of any concern to you?"

"If *you're* so reluctant to petition him, then I will do it." A crafty grin split his face. "I rather thought that I could fashion a very appealing little spiel whereby his honour or his pride might be jeopardised if he wasn't forthcoming with a little succour for his needy daughter." Looking very satisfied, he added, "And I might claim a portion of that."

"Of course there had to be something in it for you." Charity paused in the midst of a wonderful poem Hugo had composed during a couple of days spent ashore.

"I'm a businessman. Unlike your dreamy Hugo, I'm finding a practical means of solving your immediate problems. Now, what's his name?"

"I'm not telling you that."

"It's not Edwin Riverdale, by any chance?"

"How did you —?"

Cyril burst out laughing at her tone of shocked horror. "Because I see you have addressed an envelope to a gentleman of that name and, since you're desperate, this would be a likely bet."

"I wasn't going to send it."

"I think you might have to, if push came to shove. Ah, my poor girl. He will be a tough nut to crack and I suspect you'd have gone about the matter with a touch too much desperation. But I do like a challenge and am a better negotiator than you." He rose and turned for the door, reaching over to pat Charity's shoulder as he passed. "Leave matters with me. You shall hear something in the next couple of days, I promise. I feel sure there's a way we can all benefit from this mutually interesting connection. And, by the way, who was the stunner in Madame's study as I passed? I nearly fell over when I thought Lady Margaret Ponsonby was being interviewed by our most esteemed brothel-keeper. But I heard Madame call her Arabella as she slammed the door. Dead ringer for the earl's daughter, I thought I must be losing my mind."

Charity blinked in surprise and nearly

spoke unwisely before she shook her head. "I don't know.

"Well, it was dark and perhaps Lady Margaret just happened to be on my mind, being such a bosom buddy of my own sweet Miss Mabel, whom you will soon help me to woo. Because you *will* have to compromise your stubbornly held principles, my dear Charity, and start dealing with me a little more kindly if you're to save yourself from having to deal with the world's sordid problems on your back."

CHAPTER 11

"Spring is here!" Rosetta looked blooming as she blew into the breakfast room and took a seat in front of a pile of steaming crumpets. "Madame *must* be in a good mood!"

"Her daughter is home and Madame has high hopes for her," Emily said, spearing one of the rare delicacies that were usually Madame's preserve but which cook had said were for everyone, today.

"Did anyone ever *see* her daughter?" Agnes asked, her mouth full and her eyes still bleary from lack of sleep. Many girls who'd not normally make the effort to be up before noon had made an exception when they'd heard there was a table laden with good, hot food other than the usual sparse fare.

Everyone shook their heads.

"I suppose Madame doesn't want her tainted. She thinks she can set her up as better than the rest of us."

Charity blinked in surprise and nearly spoke unwisely before she shook her head in corroboration of knowing nothing.

She wondered where Arabella was now living as she reflected on Cyril's words of a few nights before. Perhaps Madame really was working behind the scenes to concoct some form of respectability for her daughter in order to see her elevated in society.

The reflection put her own sorry situation into stark relief. How was any successful kind of future to be fashioned if a girl was a bastard as she and Madame Chambon's daughter surely were? Society was unforgiving of those who transgressed.

Charity had no hope of rising above the detritus of life. She'd fallen to the lowest rung of the ladder. No one could get her out of the swamp. The best for which she could hope, quite simply, was that she'd not starve.

But Madame had connections and, clearly, her daughter Arabella was a beauty. A proud, enterprising beauty. Enterprising...unlike Charity.

"You're looking very gloomy, Charity, my dear." Madame's entrance brought a hush to the table and a guilty look to Rosetta's face as she held a half-eaten muffin in mid-air.

"Please, help yourselves, girls! Cook told you, I hope, that I'd ordered them as a special treat for you! Things are looking up, as they say." She pursed her lips into a smile that gave her heavily painted face a very prune-like look. But as her mood was clearly genial, Charity — and no doubt the rest of the girls — were relieved.

Silently they waited for her to elaborate. One didn't question Madame directly if one could help it. Charity wondered if perhaps she'd had some success on her daughter's behalf. If Madame's daughter was as beautiful and well-educated, Madame was cunning enough to pull strings in the background to set her up in a way she'd not do for the girls who made her money.

Clearly, something had pleased Madame who was only ever ebullient if business was good.

Perhaps there was a new girl arriving for whom she had high hopes.

"All of us here have felt sympathy for Charity's plight and the fact she's heard nothing from her young man in nearly four months — is that not so, Charity? Living like a scullery maid must be hard."

Charity looked around the table where the twelve girls currently working for Madame were seated. Each one of them sent her looks of sympathy. And their sentiments were genuine. A pang of gratitude swept through her. These were her true friends. Girls who had offered kind words — words of hope — when she needed them most.

Others, like Rosetta and Emily, had gone out of their way to try and effect a plan that would bring Charity the loving reunion with Hugo that she was beginning to accept was just a pipe dream.

She blinked as a wave of shame swept through her. These girls were like her in that they, too, were on society's lowest rung. They survived the only way they could — yet they could still laugh and offer mutual friendship and support.

Charity had never had to sell herself as they did every night. What right did she have to sink herself in misery and decry her lot in life?

"But now Charity, matters have become dire. Your young man has not been able to send you the maintenance he promised. I have been generous and offered you a roof over your head with little demand in return." Madame paused. "But I am not a charity, and I do apologise for the unintended pun. I, too, have rent to pay and food which must go to those who are prepared to work for it."

Charity bowed her head. Her time was up and Madame was making a public announcement of it in the least sympathetic way she knew how. It was impossible to look at the faces ranged about the table.

"So, Charity, this evening you will see a gentleman who has shown a particular interest in you."

"Not Hugo's cousin!"

Madame shook her head. "Do you really think I would be so cruel?" She made a tutting sound, as if she really did wonder that Charity could ask her such a question. "No, Mr Cyril Adams will be seeing Rosetta this evening."

A collective gasp of outrage went around the table before Madame banged on the table top for silence.

"I, in fact, suggested Rosetta since this young gentleman evinced a particular desire to be tutored by someone who would show him what would please a woman between the sheets. Apparently, he intends that Charity should help him with his penmanship, or rather, his way with words. Thanks to this unlikely quarter with what he terms his desired rehabilitation, he believes he will be a better husband than he might otherwise be were he not to gain some understanding of the potentially curious desires of his future wife."

Emily let out a derisive snort and the other girls giggled. Madame held up her hand for silence once more. "Does any girl here have a complaint against Mr Adams that I should know about?" She glanced at Rosetta. "You know I do not tolerate violence of any kind in my establishment."

"He's a selfish lover," said Emily.

"And he's parsimonious," said Ghislaine.

"And he's a cheat," muttered Molly.

Madame nodded as she silently digested this. "But he's never shown tendencies of a *vicious* nature? No? Well, that's all I need to know. The fact is, he seems to recognise that he is in need of a little tutoring, so we shall hope Rosetta can transform our Mr Adams from selfish lover to winsome bridegroom in just a few weeks."

She nodded decisively while Charity waited in trepidation for Madame to elaborate on the details of her own situation.

The time had come at last, she thought dully. Why had she not gone ahead and found an alternative situation before it was too late? She'd always been too passive. A bold, fiery girl with gumption would have found a way to survive without having to sell her body.

She stood up suddenly. "I'm not entertaining a strange gentleman. One day Hugo will come back! Whether that's in two years or five, he will find me still waiting. And I will have been true to him. I shall leave this house today, Madame. I'll find some other employment. But I will not entertain any gentleman who is not my Hugo."

Madame nodded. "Very well. No one is a prisoner here. I shall inform Mr Riverdale that you will not meet him for dinner at Claridges Hotel, after all." She pursed her lips and lifted an eyebrow. "He'll be disappointed, of course. Emily, it appears Charity will no longer be needing to borrow the new gold and cream striped gown I had made for you, after all."

～

IF HUGO HAD BEEN HERE, HE'D HAVE squeezed her hand, told her she couldn't fail to entrance him, and then he'd have borne her company to the secluded corner table between two luxuriant potted palms.

But Hugo wasn't here and Charity had only herself to rely upon.

It was a weighty responsibility. She needed to win over her father. She needed to strike the right note so that he'd not think her grasping. She had to hope he'd be overcome with fond memories of her mother, or even guilt at his abandonment of them.

What she must not do was appear desperate and needy.

At least, that's what Emily had counselled. "Be proud. Walk in with an air of assurance so that the hotel staff think you're gentry. But the moment you sit down, you must look like you're deferring to him. Be appreciative. Grateful, but not cow-towing. Respectful. A little bit in awe yet still bright and winning. Do you think you can do that?"

Charity didn't think she could at all but the moment she'd been deposited at the table by the respectable woman Madame had employed to chaperone her to such a public place, she found that, strangely, all the lessons she'd unconsciously learned about how to behave, came back to her.

"Good lord, but you're the spitting image of your mother!" the tall, handsome be-whiskered man opposite her exclaimed as he rose to greet her. And, yes, he was indeed her father. There was no mistaking the roguish look in his eye and the square-cut chin and angular nose that had first struck her when she'd been eight years old.

The fact that he said she looked like her mother sent shards of joy shooting through her. She'd heard it before but never expected to hear it again in such circumstances.

"And what a pleasure it is to finally make your acquaintance as an adult. My only child," he added, regarding her with his head on one side as a waiter handed him a menu. "Strange, but I never imagined us meeting like this. It was a shock to learn of your existence when I unexpectedly bumped into your mother all those years ago. It was on a staircase. You'd not remember it, of course, being only a little girl at the time, but…" A shadow crossed his face. "I was newly married at the time. Nevertheless, I was terribly affected by our reunion. And the knowledge I had a child."

It was not the speech she'd been expecting, though in truth Charity didn't know what she'd expected.

She didn't know what to say.

He cleared his throat. "I told your mother I'd never forgotten her. That I'd look after her. Look after you both."

Charity hadn't remembered that. But then, she'd not heard the conversation that had caused her mother to cry.

"Then…why didn't you?" she asked, resentment swelling inside.

"Your mother was too proud to become my mistress, I suppose." Her father shrugged. "Though she wavered. She nearly came with me that day. I was sorry she didn't. Of course, you'd remember nothing of this."

Charity remembered everything. Why had her mother made such a fateful decision. It hadn't brought her any joy. Charity had happily become Hugo's mistress and they'd enjoyed a deep and abiding love for nearly two years.

She felt the tears sting the back of her eyelids. Even if she had her time again she'd never wish for respectability and virtue over what she'd had with Hugo.

Her father had resumed talking. "Then, a few days ago, your friend, Mr Adams, contacted me out of the blue, told me that my daughter was in a spot of difficulty and, just as a reminder as to your identity, brandished a very competent pen and ink drawing which, he said, captured your image brilliantly. As I must say, it does."

Charity nodded in acknowledgement as she plucked at her skirts beneath the table, barely able to concentrate when the waitress came to take their order. What could she say to that? She'd expected him to deny paternity. She'd been expecting resistance. It's why she'd never had the courage to contact him before.

"I think my mother was always in love with you." Charity looked him in the eye.

"Why did you leave her the first time? She said you'd promised to marry her."

Mr Riverdale — for he'd given her no direction as to what she should call him — stroked his moustache as he gave the matter thought. "I was not the marrying kind — at the time. Quite frankly, I lied to her. I'm not proud of it." Then he smiled and Charity could see the devastating effect he must have had on her mother all those years ago. For his smile transformed him into a strikingly handsome man who seemed to have eyes only for the one upon whom he bestowed his smile. Yes, he was charming.

Dangerously so, and here was all the reason Charity had not to trust him as her mother had. Despite her high hopes, he'd bring her nothing but disappointment.

"You broke my mother's heart," Charity whispered, unable to look him in the eye and very glad that their soup had arrived.

"I'm led to believe I broke the hearts of quite a few hopeful young ladies." He picked up his soup spoon and began to eat. "However, you are, to my knowledge, my only child. My wife died last year and I've not yet been inclined to remarry though that will no doubt happen at some stage. In the meantime, it is rather a novelty to know I have a daughter. Especially such a beautiful one. Indeed, one who has garnered a good deal of novelty over the past couple of months."

Charity's tried to turn an unladylike snort into a delicate cough. "How can that be? I've barely left the house." She gathered her courage and asked, "Do you know where I live?"

"Mr Adams wouldn't tell me and, quite frankly, I don't want to know. I'm not interested in your sorry tale of penny-pinching and poverty but I am interested in what can be of benefit to both of us." He dabbed at his moustache with his napkin. "Excellent soup this. Do you like leek and cauliflower? Good. But yes, apparently your painting has garnered a reputation as a point of discussion for the young men who pass a certain hoarding on a busy street corner in Soho. Not just the men, either, I'm told."

Charity frowned, not understanding him but not interrupting as he went on,

"Usually the posters are removed or plastered over but this one — and the poster of the lovely young lady touting the benefits of her electric corset — have proved especially popular and have remained."

"What on earth can you mean? A poster on a hoarding? An electric corset?" Charity felt her face burning.

Her father leaned back in his chair and grinned, a gold eyetooth in evidence. He looked prosperous and at ease. Yet what suffering he'd caused her mother. She reigned in her resentment because she had no other choice. Only her father could save her now, it seemed.

"Yes, Mr Adams took me there and while I was admiring your excellent likeness, I was informed of these facts I've just told you by a number of the gentlemen — and some ladies, too — many of whom evinced wonder and admiration when I told them I was acquainted with the young lady. A young lady, I informed them, who was gaining quite a reputation for her piquant looks and shapely dimensions."

"Mr Riverdale, how can you tell me such

things? Patently they're not true! And it's scandalous!"

Her companion put out his hand to calm Charity though his smile had a more instant effect. "Mr Riverdale." He repeated her words, his expression quizzical. "How formal that sounds when I know, now, what you are to me. And yet, I would not have you call me father." Taking a final sip of his soup, he looked regretful. "Not in public, at least. No, I'm afraid there is no advantage to either of us in acknowledging who and what we are to one another."

Charity felt her stomach clench at his callous words. Like most men, he was interested only in how he could use her. "How could my mother have fallen in love with you?" She didn't care that this might sound the death knell to their brief relationship. The man had no moral fibre.

"Did she speak of me often?" He seemed entirely unperturbed by Charity's bitterness.

For a split-second, Charity considered rising and walking out of the dining room before she realised the consequences of such prideful behaviour.

She inhaled carefully. Hugo needed to be reassured that she was safe and she could only truly do that if she could garner some funds to tide her over the next few weeks. Regardless of what she thought of Mr Riverdale — her father — she had to be civil. She had to court his good nature and if he saw some means to profit by her it surely could not be as bad as the way Madame sought to profit by her.

"My mother spoke of you all the time. Well, on the few occasions I saw her, for of course she could not keep a child and stay in work. My grandmother housed me while I looked after a mentally deficient relative. I did that until I came to London to find work."

"Good, I was going to get to all of that. And, will return, I assure you. First, though, I truly am sorry for what your mother went through. If it's any consolation, I was deeply in love with her, too." He had the grace to at least try to look regretful. "It's true, I had mentioned marriage but this was before I came of age when my head was filled with romantic nonsense. Maybe I would have followed through but I can't be sure."

"You abandoned my mother and left to bring up a child, alone and without support!"

Mr Riverdale sent her a cautionary look. "My dear, do not berate me for what you cannot know. I had no idea your mother was pregnant when I boarded a boat for my tour of the Continent."

"She wrote!"

"I doubt my mother forwarded her letters. Listen, Charity — and goodness, that name hardly has the ring of gentility about it — marriage with your mother was not something I'd have entered into due to the inequity of our respective stations, though maybe I bandied the word around loosely in conversation with her. But I do have some scruples and I certainly wouldn't have simply abandoned her had I known about you. But I was young and foolish. Anyway, now that I have the chance to atone, I will do so."

Pique and relief swept through Charity

at the same time, followed by a wave of concern. What might she have to do in return for his assistance? He had not just offered to support her, outright, after all.

She must have been transparent for he laughed. "Your artist friend has managed to convey that pretty face of yours quite exquisitely in all your moods. Those sketches and paintings are a treasure trove. His poems and drawings of foreign lands are quite extraordinary, too, I must say."

Charity couldn't believe what he was saying. "I've seen no poems or drawings of foreign lands," she gasped. "Mr Cyril Adams has kept them from me, hasn't he? How dare he do so! He cheated Hugo, you know. You cannot believe a word he says." She paused, adding dubiously, "Though he claims to be trying to reform himself. And he did seek you out so I suppose he's been some help."

"That is a very grudging acceptance of his role in our reunification and not to be downplayed, my dear, for he has useful connections. Indeed, we both have in our respective provinces. However, to return to the part you will play, might I point out that pouting does not become you. When you finally meet and greet all of those who are mad to catch a glimpse of the mysterious Adams Girl, muse of the acclaimed artist who has been banished by his cruel father to far-flung empires where he's in danger of dying of a broken heart, you can't be adopting any such childish affectations. Now come along, flash me a smile of allure, or outrage or simple gratitude. Oh, never mind!" He picked up his knife and fork to begin on the sole that had just been put in front of him. "We have plenty of time to work on it. I'll have you coached to perfection before you are ready to face your public."

CHAPTER 12

*H*ugo removed his panama hat and slicked back his sweat-soaked hair before taking to the steps of the modest bungalow he'd called home during the one hundred miles of railway track construction he was overseeing.

Despite the heat and humidity, the last three weeks had been bearable. His uncle had been on a visit to Madras where he'd been consulting with investors of the private railway construction he and his brother had established a decade earlier.

Trade was in their blood. Maximising profits and exploiting their workers was in their blood.

But when Hugo looked at a ledger, his eyes couldn't focus.

Of course, he'd done as he'd been directed to do. He'd had little choice, after all; and none when his uncle had been in residence. Eight months in the sun, on horseback and on foot, overseeing the painstaking laying of hundreds of miles of railway track had browned his skin and given him strength and bulk.

His footsteps provided the signal for the household servants to begin the evening ritual that brought some relief after his daily rigours and as he stepped onto the verandah the punkawallah was in place with his fan while his gin and tonic was brought in on a tray.

For the past few weeks, the servants hadn't been so assiduously punctual but their master was expected any minute. Their real master. The one who paid their wages, beat them when they did not please him and turned them out onto the streets on a whim.

Hugo had as much fear and contempt of Septimus Adams as any of his Indian staff.

But fortunately, his uncle was not yet returned and he could enjoy a quiet drink in contemplation of the beautiful sunset and reflection of what he'd left behind in England.

A small boy trailing after his mother on the front lawn as she picked twigs from the ground captured his attention. When Hugo noticed the monkey observing them from above, he knew he had to sketch the scene.

It wasn't often that his fingers weren't itching to record some amusing vignette, or to paint the magical colours of this overwhelming country.

He rose and went to the large desk where he kept his writing and painting implements. Of course, he had to conduct another search for any correspondence that might have been delivered while he'd been out. But there was nothing, only a pile of business letters addressed to his uncle, including one in his father's hand.

Hugo stared at it. A ship had delivered the latest post from England but, again, there was nothing from Charity.

It didn't make sense. She couldn't have

forgotten him so quickly when every minute of every day an image of her sweet face sustained him throughout whatever unpalatable task he must perform in his father and uncle's mercantile interests.

For a moment he just stood staring at the neatly stacked piles of correspondence awaiting his uncle's attention. There would be profit and loss statements, invitations to social events, requests for business consideration. All the day to day matters that meant nothing to Hugo while in his hand he clutched the simple parchment and charcoal that gave his existence meaning.

Actually, these were just the outward manifestations of any meaning. When it came to the true and deep nourishment of his soul, he needed the warm, human connection of the only good person who'd ever touched his life.

He needed Charity.

The vision of her that swam before his eyes was so real and intense, he thought he was being possessed by the devil when it dissolved the moment he reached out a hand to grasp it.

That's how it was with dreams.

With a cry of frustration, he flung his arms wide before covering his face with his hands. The sketching materials flew into the air and hit the wall, falling to the floor as Hugo sank to his knees.

What was wrong with him? It had been nine months since he'd seen his beloved and every day only increased his torment. In the darkness of his thoughts, she continually returned to him, her expression at first shy, then gaining in confidence before she held out her arms to draw him to her breast.

But she wasn't here. And Hugo had no idea how she was faring. All he could do was send her his wages, which he channelled through a trusted servant to bypass his uncle. Until he heard back from Charity that his support was no longer needed, he'd keep sending her money for what else was going to keep her from the streets?

What else but his assistance would save her from that which terrified her more than anything else: becoming like Madame Chambon's other girls.

The soft tread of a servant brought him

to his senses. Wearily he rose, casting about for his scattered tools of trade. He'd sketch to keep the demons at bay.

The boy and his mother were gone but Charity's vision could be conjured up with ease. He'd take his paper and his charcoal, relax in a cane chair on the verandah where the afternoon breeze cooled him after a day of physical exertion, and he'd do what he loved. He'd find peace and try to keep at bay the knowledge that he still had to endure another year here before he was his own man.

Placing his parchment on the table surface, he glanced towards the desk and saw his piece of charcoal wedged between it and the wall. He went back, crouching down so he could run his hand along the gap until it encountered resistance.

But as his fingers grasped the object, it was not a drawing implement he withdrew but a letter.

Unopened, he saw as he held it up.

And addressed to him in Charity's hand.

The pounding of his heart was loud in his ears as he returned to his private nook on the verandah, ripping the envelope with no finesse in his haste to learn the most up-to-date information to be had about the girl he loved.

But upon scanning the date, he realised this had not come in the last post only to have inadvertently slipped off the desk and out of sight.

It had been written five months before, just as Charity was preparing to embrace the spring.

With terror and foreboding, he soon discovered, as he scanned the lines of tiny writing.

By God, Cyril had been pestering her, persuading her of the comforts he could provide Charity if Hugo failed to live up to his promises to send her what meagre financial assistance he could.

He couldn't stay seated, such was his anger and agitation.

Cyril was a snake in the grass and Hugo had been a fool to have taken at face value the lie that his motivation in cheating and ruining his cousin was simply so he'd not be the one to accompany his father to India.

No, Cyril had always had his eye on the main chance. And with Hugo out of the way, he thought he could make a play for Charity. Not just because Charity was the girl Hugo loved but because Charity was pure and untainted by the grubbiness of life and there was some perverse streak in Cyril that made him want to sully whatever goodness came his way.

"Hot in the sun, eh?"

He'd not heard his uncle enter the room and he looked up with undisguised loathing as the older man removed his panama hat as he made for a cane chair.

Hugo stepped forward, brandishing the letter under his uncle's nose as if it were a weapon.

"How many more of these have you kept from me?" he asked softly. It was not often his temper rose to the fore with such fire and fury. But he had to contain himself. His uncle had a mind that worked like his father's. He enjoyed outbursts because he was in a position to quell them swiftly and effectively. He was physically stronger and he controlled the finances.

Hugo took stock, realising how much his own physique had changed compared to a year ago. Since the Christmas they'd left, age had diminished his uncle. His hair was thinning, and more white than gray as it had been when they'd arrived in this country. He seemed to have shrunk, physically.

Meanwhile, though Hugo was not exactly strapping, he was, without doubt, stronger, more powerful than his uncle. And he could feel the urge to use this newfound strength; to do violence, tingling in his fingertips.

But violence would achieve nothing. It was not going to give him the answers he demanded right now. His uncle was obdurate and wily. He liked to taunt and he'd taunt Hugo by withholding the information Hugo was so desperate for, unless Hugo played him just right.

Any suggestion that Hugo might resort to his recently acquired physical strength would be fatal.

Generally, Hugo had as little to do with his uncle as he could. They often spent their evenings apart, his uncle socialising with several chosen acquaintances nearby. Hugo could imagine it gave him secret pleasure each time the post was delivered, to withhold, or destroy, any correspondence addressed to his nephew.

But surely the time would come when it would be more satisfying to taunt Hugo with everything he'd had the power to deny him?

His uncle peered at the letter Hugo held out as if he were trying to place it.

"Ah yes, the writing. A very pretty, feminine hand. Extremely accomplished for such a creature, too." He sent Hugo a benign smile.

"So, you knew who was writing to me." Hugo tried to ignore the insult to Charity. "And you deliberately kept *only* her letters from me, I assume, since I've received the regular, expected missives from my father, exhorting me to do my duty. Yes, there's been no shortage of the letters that crow about the company's trading success, the recognition that's finally coming your way, the hopes for an investiture becoming an increasing reality. Meanwhile, any comfort that may be coming my way is withheld as if I'm an errant schoolboy who can't be trusted not to tarnish the precious reputation. Can't be trusted not to give into his base impulses like you did, Uncle; and my father did, when you both could have married heiresses or aristocrats who'd have erased the taint of trade and elevated the family a notch or ten. I've heard it a thousand times."

Septimus's nostrils flared but he kept his temper. He was better at that than Hugo's father. The less fiery brother, perhaps, but he enjoyed sticking the knife in. His methods of torture were more sophisticated for he had crafted subtlety to a degree Hugo's father had not.

"And it's the truth. Money is the currency that brings us the trappings of the good life but it's the perception of good breeding that opens the real doors." Septimus reached for the gin and tonic that had just been offered him on a tray by a servant, passing silently through the room, and indicated the room with a wave of his arm. "A little bit of discomfort brings a lifetime of rewards. Soon I'll return to England with a healthy balance sheet to show for my efforts. Meanwhile, you will thank your father and I for curbing the impulses that are natural to a young man who believes himself in the throes of love. I was young once, believe it or not, and I believed that what I felt for Cyril's mother was love. Of course it wasn't. Your father made the same mistake I did."

"I am not like you or my father." God, how good it was to know it.

"You believe you are purer of heart and that elevates you above the rest of us. Yes, Hugo, I know that's what you think. I know your sort. I don't understand you but I know what's good for you and you'll thank me for it when your little obsession has run its course and you can choose a wife when you are no longer in the throes of calf love. A wife who will add worth to the family name."

Hugo shook his head. "You had no right to keep Charity's letters from me. Not when I did what was expected and accompanied you here for the sake of the company."

"No, for your sake, Hugo." Septimus stroked his moustache. "And if you want re-assurance regarding Charity's well-being, Cyril writes that he's taking good care of her in your absence."

Hugo stiffened but did not take the bait. He knew his uncle was lying. "Charity loathes Cyril. She knows he cheated me at the gaming table. She knows Cyril encouraged me to be a fool, to get drunk and to play deep, thinking I was securing my future when really it was my father's plan to keep me financially dependent upon him for another two years."

Septimus took a leisurely sip of his drink. "Cyril was persuaded to act in your best interests, Hugo." He picked up the wedge of lemon and gave it a squeeze. "No need to sound so bitter. He was acting in *all* of our best interests, for you are decidedly better suited to doing what needs to be done for the business in this god-forsaken country than Cyril who, besides, was to come into his inheritance a good deal earlier than you. He's far less reliable than you when it comes to sticking to his guns. Cyril takes his pleasure without being troubled by his conscience." He took another sip then added, thoughtfully, "Though it seems it was his conscience that persuaded him to offer your young lady his protection in the absence of any other form of maintenance."

"I've sent her all my wages," Hugo muttered, turning away, sickened by the conversation. "She has no need of Cyril's protection so stop pretending to me that my Charity isn't as faithful as Homer's Penelope."

"My dear boy, your wages have been going straight into the Bank of India." Septimus evinced surprise. "I thought you knew that. Or perhaps I neglected to tell you how assiduous your faithful manservant has been in keeping me informed of your state of mind. Yes, I know you wrote a letter of direction for a large portion to be directed to an account in London which I presumed could be accessed by your young lady but in your best interests I overrode this." He patted his chest. "I couldn't let matters of the heart blight your future. Of course, when you have reached your twenty-fifth birthday in a year's time and are free to do as you wish with your grandfather's inheritance, you'll be able to supplement your new wealth with *all* your hard-won earnings." He smiled. "You'll even be able to go home and marry your young lady if you truly wish. If she's waited that long for you." Although his tone remained genial, his eyes hardened. "But you can rest assured that, in the meantime, Cyril has been looking after her with all the tender care you'd have lavished upon her, yourself, had you been there." He raised his eyebrows. "No need to look so concerned, Hugo, my boy. I know the idea of giving or accepting charity can be hurtful to one's notions of pride, and your sensibilities are highly developed. So, don't regard it as *charity*. Cyril won't be out of pocket for attending to her daily needs. I'm sure she's paying for it in the only way she knows how."

Instinctively, Hugo raised his arm. He wanted to belt his uncle so badly his whole body shook with the effort of resisting the impulse. But he had to drop his arm and close his eyes. He had to rein in his rage. It would not satisfy his screaming desire for vengeance, or ease his terrible fear.

He turned away.

How had Charity survived for seven months without a penny from Hugo? How could he blame her if she'd succumbed to Cyril's advances? But again, how could he *not* forgive her for whatever she'd had to do to survive? In her letter, she'd told him how hard she'd tried to find work as a servant but that it was impossible without a reference from a current, respectable employer. She'd told him how relieved and grateful she was for the money he'd promised to send. And Hugo had taken comfort in the belief that, though small, the amounts he thought he was sending her were keeping her safe until he got back.

He kept his eyes closed. The rage would not abate. His world was black, his ears full of the distress he had to hold tight.

The information that Charity had not received a penny from him since her last, fearful and desperate letter, was enough to send him insane.

Slowly, he exhaled, then quietly and with deliberate care, he walked past his uncle.

"What *are* you doing?"

Hugo paused in the midst of gathering writing materials from the desk and putting them into his satchel. "I'm leaving tonight. Now, in fact."

"Good lord, boy! I'd never have told you if I knew you'd be so...juvenile in your response." Septimus glanced across the room as if to emphasise the pitch dark that had fallen so suddenly beyond the shutters. A servant had lit lamps in the meantime and the smell of spiced food wafted from the distant kitchen.

"In the morning we can talk about this. Yes, you're a man, not a boy, and entitled to free will but your father would never forgive me if I let you jeopardise everything we've been working towards. The company's future growth and prospects. Your future growth and prospects."

Hugo ignored him. He fastened the clasps of the satchel and reached for his hat which he'd tossed onto a side table.

"For God's sake, be reasonable, Hugo."

His uncle sounded rattled. Hugo didn't acknowledge him as he evaded his grasping hand on the way to the door. "Hugo! If you walk away now, you walk away from everything your grandfather has left in trust for you to receive in just a matter of months!"

Behind him, he could hear Septimus's footsteps on the soft runner, Hugo's final journey that led from this hated prison. "Hugo, don't be a fool! Think with your head, for once!"

Hugo turned on the front verandah. The wide, shuttered expanse was illuminated by the waxy yellow glow from the lamps placed around the perimeter. He thought how much he'd like to paint Charity reclining against the pile of cushions upon the low bench by the far wall. The light would imbue her chestnut hair with a glorious lustre, highlighting that creamy complexion of hers. He thought of how he might find her when he returned. With Cyril? Another man? Many other men?

He didn't care.

"I no longer care about my inheritance." His heart quickened. He took the first step into the inky blackness. He'd send a servant to fetch the trunk from his room, packed with his belongings.

"Hugo!"

Hugo ignored him. "There comes a time when one must stop thinking with one's head." He didn't care if his uncle was out of earshot though he could hear Septimus's footsteps nearing the edge of the verandah. He turned and spoke into the darkness, uncaring whether his uncle heard him or not. "When one must think with one's heart and one's conscience."

Like a wraith, the night embraced him. "I've realised it's the only way I can live with myself," he muttered as he walked away.

CHAPTER 13

"It strikes just the right note, Charity. Perfect!" Madame Chambon circled Charity with a critical eye though her mouth was curved into a smile. "What gentleman will not want to devour you but he will have to think such thoughts inside, no? You are not just anyone's."

"Charity! Mr Riverdale is here!"

Charity pinched her lips and clasped her hands together, swinging around for a final beseeching look at Madame. "Is it a mistake?" she asked.

"A mistake?" Madame cocked an eyebrow as she smiled, though her expression was tinged with sadness. "How wonderful if

I could accompany you. A woman like me, however, could never gain entry to such society. Besides, half the gentlemen there tonight would know me."

"Charity! He says you'll be late!"

Charity took a few steps towards the door then turned back towards Madame. "Arabella will be magnificent. I'll tell you everything that happens, every gentleman who engages her!"

"It is not Arabella's night to shine," said Madame. "Tonight will only prove if she can survive in a snake pit. It is her testing time but it is *your* moment to triumph over your past. Now go! Mr Riverdale is waiting."

She did not call him her father, just as Charity had never called him her father. But he had been assiduous in following through everything that he had promised that first night at dinner.

First the drawings, the paintings had been disseminated, placed in prominent places, in news sheets, magazines, usually with a snippet of verse, a teaser. Words that Hugo had used to describe Charity; his love for her; the essence of her.

She'd become a talking point. An enigma. An icon.

Oh, her father had managed it so well. As if he were born to tease, just as he'd done so successfully with her mother. His real line of work had been more prosaic. A desultory interest in a publishing firm established by his grandfather and which he used to visit if he had the inclination to go to work that morning.

But since making Charity's acquaintance it seemed he'd been inspired by work rather than visiting his club.

"Perfect! Just perfect!" Her father smiled approvingly as he opened the door of the carriage that waited for them around the corner. "Your Madame Chambon has a good eye. And she's a woman of the utmost discretion. Why, how many entrances are there to that building, including underground. No spy could run you to ground there. But soon you will be moving out, Charity, my dear. This is no place for a girl like you. Tonight will change everything. You'll see."

Charity shifted uncomfortably. "I don't

want to move out. Not until my Hugo comes back and I can live with him. As his wife."

Her father patted her knee. "And when did you last hear from your Hugo?"

Charity didn't answer though her throat thickened. Her father knew very well she'd heard nothing since several weeks after Hugo's departure.

Still, she held out hope. There was some very good reason for his silence. Not once did she despair and believe he'd forsaken her. She knew Hugo too well.

"And now we are here. My! The welcome party is bigger than I'd expected." He sounded taken aback, which was surprising. Nothing seemed to faze Mr Riverdale.

Charity took a constricted breath. She was sure she'd not laced her corset too tightly when Madame's maid had dressed her but suddenly, she was finding it hard to breathe. She touched the rose at her decolletage and plucked at the bows and furbelows of her train as she stepped out of the carriage at their destination, rearranging her bustle.

Cyril was waiting at the bottom of the stairs. He grinned at her as he offered his arm. "Smile like a princess, not a startled rabbit," he whispered. "Everyone here wants to see the girl pictured in the book. Not some frightened hopeful."

"But there are so many people." Charity took a lungful of air as she gazed at the faces ranged around her, eager and smiling, some reaching out hands to touch her. "I wasn't expecting this. It's only supposed to be the launch of Hugo's book."

"But Hugo's book has become the sensation of the season, my dear. It is the only thing anyone wants this Christmas." He raised her hand to the crowd, then kissed it, and a cheer rang out. "See! They want you to be happy."

"But they mistake what they see." Anxiously, Charity turned to her father on her other side, and he patted her shoulder, catching her words.

"What they choose to read into any interaction is their affair, not yours," he said, matching his pace to hers as she negotiated the stairs with all the elegance she could muster in her tightly fitting cuirass and the heavy, elegant upholstery that followed her like a sinuous snake. "You know that it is Hugo's work that has made this evening possible and you will tell the world that. The truth will always out."

The truth will always out. Charity glanced at the two men on either side of her. Men she had once despised. Men who had sought to profit from her. Men whose company she had come to enjoy as their curious experiment had gathered momentum, fuelling them with excitement and genuine pride in the achievements of cousin on Cyril's part and daughter on Mr Riverdale's part.

Tonight Hugo would be publicly revealed to the anticipatory gathering as the author of *Tales of Love and Loss,* his wildly successful book of poems and accompanying paintings and drawings. Charity was merely here as his muse. But she was a face everyone now recognised.

"Miss Charity, please can you sign this?" A shy young man hovering amidst a group of eager-eyed young people near the entrance approached her holding a print of one of Hugo's drawings of her.

"When will your young man return to England?" asked another. "You must miss him very much. That cruel and wicked father who forced you apart is not here, is he?"

She'd heard such sentiments with increasing frequency, lately. It seemed Mr Riverdale had done a good job of imbuing her life with mystery and pathos. While her early years were shrouded in ambiguity, he'd made much of the star-crossed lovers theme.

Tonight's attendees seemed to find the story as compelling as Hugo's talent.

"Not much longer," her father encouraged her, during a brief interlude when Charity's attention wasn't being sought. "Cyril will look after you when I'm on stage to officiate over the launch. You'll feel much more relaxed when the formalities are over." He squeezed her hand as he prepared to leave her. "My, my Charity, you have surprised me." His look was admiring. "You were such a mouse when you agreed to meet me all those months ago. Albeit a very beautiful mouse. But you have grown into your role as if you were made for it."

"I hate every minute of it," Charity confessed with a smile, taking a sip of her champagne. "But I'm very grateful for there are other things I'd hate more."

She felt herself color as she realised the implications of what she'd said.

"You will make a fine consort for your Hugo when he finally returns to you." Her father obviously chose to ignore her earlier inference.

"What if he doesn't come back?"

There was a silence. "Do you know, that is the first time I've ever heard you voice doubt. Tonight, of all nights."

Charity bowed her head. "You make me ashamed of myself. If Hugo doesn't come back, it's because he cannot. But in his absence, he has given me the greatest gift." She raised her head and looked about her. Jewels and sumptuous clothing adorned all those who'd crowded into the large reception room. There were artists rubbing shoulders with duchesses, oil magnates and publishing moguls hobnobbing with actresses.

"He's given me a place in the world," she said. "A place where I can be proud of who I am."

"He's made you the most sought-after woman in all of London town," said Cyril, coming around to her other side and raising her hand to his lips. "Here's to our *cause celebre* as her benefactor takes to the stage and sings the praises of my cousin." He cocked one eyebrow and sent Charity his most lascivious look. "Of whom I am insanely jealous."

Charity tossed her head. "But who is soon to wed the lovely Miss Dermot — thanks in part to me, I might add — who is heading this way flanked by, if I'm not mistaken, Lady Margaret Ponsonby...." She dropped her voice to a whisper, and added, "if one didn't know any better."

CHAPTER 14

*I*t was as if he were still aboard a rocking boat. Hugo stepped out of the carriage and nearly fell flat on his face. Though he was exhausted from the rough and gruelling crossing, nothing was going to stop him seizing Charity and taking her home to safety.

Yes, he'd forgo his inheritance. He'd have to work hard to earn a living any way he could. But he was a man of education and, somehow, he could provide for two people.

He ran the back of his hand across his eyes and prayed for the strength to do what he had to do.

But try as he might, he could not rid

himself of the anger that had been sim-
mering since his parting from his uncle.
It seemed it wasn't enough for Cyril to
ruin Hugo and see him banished. Now,
Cyril had stolen Charity from him after
helping ensure she'd been made
destitute.

Through the actions of Cyril's own father. And with Hugo's own father as an ac-
complice.

For a moment Hugo could only stare at
the grand edifice, the assembly hall Emily
had said Charity had been taken to for some
grand entertainment.

"With Cyril Adams?" Hugo had asked
her, barely able to focus on her face due to
his swimming vision.

"Yes, Mr Adams will be there," she'd said
as he'd stumbled down the steps, ignoring
her cries that he didn't seem to understand;
suggesting he was feverish, that perhaps he
should rest rather than hunt down Charity
in such a state.

Hunt down Charity? Was she suggesting
that in only one year his beloved could have
switched allegiance so that Hugo was

hunting her down rather than seeking her out?

He staggered a little and a gentleman assisting a lady from the carriage that had drawn up by the front steps sent him a disapproving look before shepherding his companion indoors.

The warmth that hit him as a pair of footmen opened the double doors onto the disorienting spectacle was like a furnace when he was already burning up.

It took a few moments to see straight. The room seemed to be swimming in and out of focus.

He was surprised at how quiet everything was when there were so many people here. Then he realised someone was on stage, speaking. He glanced up at the gentleman, a distinguished-looking man who seemed to have the crowd in thrall, and who stood beside a drawing which, he realised with a start was of Charity.

Hugo tried to attend to what he was saying but he caught only the words "my daughter" which seemed to create something of a sensation. He could sense the emotion around him but he couldn't understand anything, least of all why the gentleman should be standing on stage surrounded by paintings Hugo had drawn.

He shook his head, for of course he was dreaming, and then saw the man hold out his arm to indicate someone, at which point the crowd parted and he could see, as clearly as if she stood in a halo of sunshine, his beloved Charity.

She looked like a goddess in a sheath of white silk adorned with blue velvet ribbons and his heart swelled as he saw her smile.

But she wasn't smiling at him, he now saw. She was smiling at Cyril who was raising her hand to his lips.

For a moment Hugo felt suspended above reality.

Everything was a dream. It had to be.

Until a waft of cool air from the doors opening behind him brought him face to face with this cruel world, and pain like he'd never felt before seared his heart. Swaying as his hopes fragmented into a million shards, he realised the futility of his life from here on towards meaningless eternity.

He reached out for something to balance him but there was nothing. He was as alone as he'd been before he met Charity.

And ever would be, now that he'd discovered his love had been in vain.

Frozen to the spot, swaying as his vision coalesced into hues of scarlet and black, he confronted his options.

He could either quietly leave and never see Charity again, ceding her to Cyril, the man who had won. Again.

That would be the path of nobility. He'd make no fuss. He'd sink into quiet obscurity, just as he'd lived his whole life. In his father and cousin's shadow. A disappointment. The boy who simply wasn't up to scratch.

Or he could make his feelings quite clear and direct, before walking out of Charity's life.

Leaving her the option to follow if she chose.

He drew his shoulders back. The crowd had broken into applause but were quiet now. Hugo had no idea what the man on stage was saying, and he didn't care.

All he cared about was navigating to

where Cyril stood with his bland, unctuous expression, thinking he could possess Charity. Thinking he could walk roughshod over Hugo as he had all his life.

Hugo managed to cross the carpeted expanse without falling over. That was one small victory.

"Cyril."

The moment his cousin turned, Hugo raised his fist and clipped him across the jaw.

The satisfaction of seeing the horror on Cyril's expression was short-lived, swallowed up as it was by the sound of his Charity's scream.

And then, neatly, and quietly, Hugo crumpled to the floor, disappearing into merciful oblivion.

CHAPTER 15

Sunshine sparkling on a carpet of snow was one of the most beautiful sights Charity had ever seen as she looked through the window of her attic room for the last time while Emily laced her into her dress.

She heard Madame's heavy tread on the stairs and turned, but for once her body did not go rigid with fear.

"*Ma cherie*, you are a picture of purity!" Madame swept forward and, for the first time in Charity's adult life, she was embraced in a motherly hug. "I knew this day would come! That you would be my first real success!"

"You did?"

Madame nodded as she occupied herself with tweaking the folds and ruffles of Charity's exquisite wedding gown.

"From the moment I saw the love between you and Mr Hugo, I knew you'd be my first girl to step directly from my establishment and into the arms of society."

Charity didn't want to suggest that Madame was reviewing the past year through rose-coloured glasses. There had been many times Charity had feared Madame was about to sell her to the highest bidder.

"Even when Mr Hugo didn't write for more than six months and Charity had not a bean to live on?" Emily asked as she arranged Charity's curls, emboldened, clearly, by Madame's unusually expansive mood.

"I'll admit I harboured doubts about Mr Hugo. Not his fidelity, for my dears, I have never seen a young man more desperately in love. Why, I believe he'd even give up his art for you, Charity."

"But his art is what saved Charity," said Emily between a mouthful of hair pins.

"No." Charity shook her head. "Hugo's love did that."

She remembered, with emotion, that extraordinary night when Cyril had escorted her to the launch of Hugo's book.

When her father had stood on stage, surrounded by paintings and drawings Hugo had created — not just of Charity, but scenes of daily life in India, sweet vignettes of the children, and exquisite pictures of sunsets — she'd never felt prouder.

That is, until the man she'd never called anything other than Mr Riverdale, the man whose zeal and enthusiasm she admired, whose kindness — not apparent, initially — she'd come to appreciate, had publicly acknowledged her.

She'd never forget the sense of unreality she'd felt as he paused, indicated Hugo's paintings, then said to a hushed audience, "It is to this young artist, who cannot be here tonight, that I owe the greatest debt. *Not* just because early indications suggest that this book will be Riverdale & Son's greatest commercial success. But because Mr Hugo Adams' talent has reunited me with someone I had thought lost to me forever. Someone I have grown to love, very dearly. Someone I might never have seen again had his drawings not revealed the identity of..."

Charity's pulse had quickened when she heard this. She'd bitten her lip until she tasted blood, releasing her pent-up breath in a cry of disbelief when he'd finished, "my beautiful, kind, ever-forgiving long-lost daughter, Charity."

Her body still thrummed with the extraordinary joy of being accepted by her father and being reunited with her lover. Within minutes. Certainly, those few moments had had their problems but, if nothing else, her father had proved himself a magician when it came to turning a potentially disastrous moment of confrontation and sensation into a moment that seemed to have cemented the adoration of a hitherto merely curious and admiring public.

He'd also artfully whitewashed Charity's past.

"Ah, Charity, *mon petit chou*! You are a sight for sore eyes. Are you ready?"

Charity nodded at Madame, her hand on the older woman's arm as she was led towards the establishment's secret entrance, via a staircase and tunnel that went beneath the cobbled street and exited from an innocuous row of dwellings where Charity knew her carriage would be waiting.

Indeed, there was Cyril beside the handsome equipage, his reception full of admiration.

"You look like an angel. Or a princess." He swept his arm wide. "Can you hear them singing about you and Hugo?"

Charity put her head on one side to listen to the pure notes of a group of carollers, children mostly, standing just across the road, singing *Joy to the World*. They'd reached the third verse and the words spoke to her heart:

"No more let sins and sorrows grow,
Nor thorns infest the ground;

He comes to make His blessing flow
Far as the curse is found,
Far as the curse is found,
Far as, far as the curse is found."

"*Joy to the world*," Charity repeated, thoughtfully, as she put her foot on the bottom of the carriage steps. "I hope you're feeling it, too, Cyril. And that your jaw isn't too sore."

"Oh, Hugo was too sick and weak to do much damage," he said, carelessly, touching the spot where Hugo's fist had collected with his face three weeks earlier. "Which is just as well. Now that he's quite recovered, I can see that Mabel might have been peevish if I'd spoiled the wedding photographs for her."

"Mabel could never be peevish. She's too nice for that!" said Charity with a laugh, thinking how marvellous it was that she'd be able to publicly attend Cyril's wedding in two weeks' time with Hugo. They'd decided to delay their own wedding trip for the event.

"And much too nice for me since she's

forgiven me everything. I really don't deserve her." He was suddenly too serious for Charity's liking when Charity felt close to bursting with happiness.

"*Everything?*" she asked playfully with arched eyebrow.

He had the grace to look uncomfortable. "I admitted to the gambling and the cheating. Only on two significant occasions, I might add, though I was guilty of a few threats, having learned early how to make others afraid of me when, really, I was no threat at all. Father was a good model." With a rueful smile, he added, "The only part I haven't told her was about Rosetta. And, really, I was paying Rosetta to help me be what Mabel would want. You won't tell her? Mabel, I mean?"

Charity laughed at his alarm. "I shall tell no lies but I shall not volunteer anything, if that's what you're worried about. Now, the carollers have moved on and there's nothing keeping us here. I suggest it's time I meet my father if he's to get me to the church in time. Hugo might think I'm not coming and decide to go away again."

~

FOR THE THIRD TIME IN FIVE MINUTES, HUGO glanced at his timepiece.

Cyril patted him on the shoulder. "She hadn't changed her mind when I saw her half an hour ago."

"You definitely deposited her safely with her father?" Hugo couldn't remember feeling this agitated, ever.

"I did. And he was as excited as she was at the prospect of coming here."

"She was excited?"

Cyril rolled his eyes. "Lord, Hugo, but you always were exasperating."

"Hush! I think she's here!"

Hugo twisted his neck, tingles of excitement shooting through his extremities as the door opened and the organ began to play. The church was filled to capacity, but he barely glanced at the rows of well-dressed ladies and gentlemen who were here for what had been touted as the most intriguing and anticipated event of the season.

Two people who were not in attendance,

and who would not be missed, were Hugo's father and uncle.

Mr Riverdale had not shied away from citing their cruelty towards son and nephew as the reason for denying the two young lovers what they longed for and what they deserved. He'd woven their roles into a tale that tugged at the heartstrings and, with its virtuous heroine, talented, driven and hard-done-by hero, together with the evil, controlling, manipulative relatives, made excellent news copy.

Didn't the public love a reason for displaying strong emotion, whether love or disapproval? No, Septimus and Thomas Adams would not have been welcome in church that day.

Hugo held his breath as Charity stepped into the church, at first a dark, mysterious figure with the sunlight at her back. A snippet of competing song made his ears prick up. A band of carollers was singing *Joy to the World*, and his heart swelled before the door closed behind Charity and her father, and Charity became, in the dim light of London's most fashionable church, a figure of breathtaking poise and beauty as she slowly progressed up the aisle on her father's arm.

A young woman whose smile radiated all the love and forgiveness and goodness that was the essence of her being.

That was what had sustained him through the long, empty year he'd been away from her.

Briefly, he gripped her hand. "You waited for me." His voice felt hoarse with emotion.

"I never doubted you'd be back to keep your promise," she whispered as she settled herself at his side in front of the parson who cleared his throat, ready to begin the ceremony that would bind them together, forever, as husband and wife. "And a year early, too." She gave his hand one last squeeze before dropping it, adding the words that reflected the sentiments that had sustained him through such pain and hardship.

"Though I'd have waited a lifetime."

THE END

CHISTMAS CHARITY IS BOOK 5 IN MY *FAIR Cyprians of London* series about a group of enterprising young women enticed through trickery or desire to work for a high-class London House of Assignation in the 1870s. I hope you enjoyed it!

Dangerous Gentlemen
The Mysterious Governess
Beyond Rubies
Lady Unveiled: The Cuckold's Conspiracy

GEORGIAN MYSTERY ROMANCE Series
Wicked Wager
Her Valentine's Secret

FAIR CYPRIANS OF LONDON Series
Saving Grace
Forsaking Hope
Keeping Faith
Wedding Violet
Christmas Charity

ABOUT THE AUTHOR

Beverley Oakley, an Australian author who grew up in the African mountain kingdom of Lesotho, emigrated to South Australia when she was young, and married a Norwegian bush pilot she met while managing a safari lodge in Botswana's Okavango Delta.

Beverley writes historical romance laced with mystery, scandal and intrigue. She lives north of Melbourne (overlooking a fabulous Gothic lunatic asylum) with the same gorgeous Norwegian husband, two daughters and a rambunctious Rhodesian Ridgeback.

Browse Beverley's books, on Amazon.

Visit Beverley's website - www.
beverleyoakley.com - to sign up for her
newsletter (and receive a free book)
Join Beverley's reader group on Facebook

Follow Beverley
On Bookbub
On Goodreads
On Facebook